WAR AT NUGGET CREEK

WAR AT NUGGET CREEK

by

Wayne C. Lee

The Golden West Large Print Books
Long Preston, North Yorkshire,
BD23 4ND, England.

British Library Cataloguing in Publication Data.

Lee, Wayne C.
    War at Nugget Creek.

      A catalogue record of this book is
      available from the British Library

      ISBN   978-1-84262-910-9 pbk

First published 1985

Copyright © 1985 by Wayne C. Lee

Cover illustration © Michael Thomas

The moral right of the author has been asserted

Published in Large Print 2012 by arrangement with
Golden West Literary Agency

The Golden West Large Print is an imprint of Library Magna
Books Ltd.

Printed and bound in Great Britain by
T.J. (International) Ltd., Cornwall, PL28 8RW

CHAPTER ONE

The sun was no more than an hour from setting when Dan York rode into Goldtown. The place looked peaceful enough, but somewhere near here York's father and stepmother had died not long ago. Because of their deaths, he was here now.

He pulled up at the hitchrack in front of the Lucky Strike Saloon just beyond the hotel. Dan's experience as a miner, freight-wagon driver, and cowboy had taught him that in most towns a saloon was the best place for a newcomer to get all kinds of information.

He stepped into the gloomy interior and up to the bar. A heavy, bald-headed man behind the bar moved over to fasten icy blue eyes on him.

'What will it be, mister?'

'Information,' York said. 'I'm looking for Sam Frake's ranch.'

The two miners standing close to York suddenly stopped their chatter and stared at him. Their silence seemed to spread like the plague over the room. It became so quiet that a quarter dropped on the far end of the bar to pay for some drinks sounded like a heavy shovel slammed against a rock.

York ran his eyes over those close to him, meeting stony stares. Then he came back to the ice-blue eyes of the bartender. He held his gaze until the bartender dropped his eyes.

'Nobody asks to see Sam Frake,' the bartender said finally, looking at York again.

'What do you want to see him for?' a man down the bar demanded.

York turned to stare at a muscular man whose brown eyes held the ferocity of a mountain lion. York seldom saw a man as big as he himself was, but this man came close. He wasn't quite as tall as York's six feet four inches, but he was almost as heavy.

'It's not Sam Frake I want to see,' York said evenly. 'It's Carlita Frake, and I'm guessing I'll find her on the Frake ranch.'

'Sam Frake's ranch is up beyond Nugget,' the bartender said uneasily, his eyes flipping from York to the brown-eyed man. 'That's up Nugget Creek five or six miles.'

'The Frakes ain't inviting company,' the big man at the bar said, sweeping two men back so he could face York. 'Just what do you want with Carlita Frake?'

A warning surged through York. A warning to avoid a fight. But he certainly had no intention of stating his business to this proddy giant. Dan was wearing boots and Levi's like a cowman, and here in the Lucky

Strike, he looked out of place among these miners.

York had seen the mines dotting the mountainside northeast of town. He had spotted a ranch to the southwest of town in the big valley. He had hoped that would be Frake's ranch but, according to the bartender, it wasn't.

'My business is with Carlita Frake,' York said, meeting the man's fiery glare.

'I'm making it my business. You may think you're too big a man to be told anything. But I'm telling you to speak up.'

'Take it easy, Flash,' the bartender said. 'He ain't doing no harm.'

'He ain't going to, either, Al,' the big man retorted, never taking his eyes off Dan York. 'Who are you, mister?'

'The name is Dan York.' He turned toward the door. He'd learned what he'd come in here for.

The big man called Flash stepped over and blocked York's path. 'You're not going anywhere till I'm through with you,' he snapped.

Dan stilled the throbbing in his head. He'd always had to battle his impulsiveness. Right now his impulse was to knock the arrogance out of this peacock.

'Do you figure on stopping me?' York asked softly.

'Yeah,' Flash said. 'Just like this.'

He threw a fist at York. York barely had time to jerk his head sideways, and that released all the fury he'd been holding back. Due to his height, Dan York looked thin and lean, but he tipped the scales at two hundred and twenty pounds. And he knew how to make the most of every ounce.

Dan's fist smashed against the side of Flash's jaw. Flash reeled backward, caught himself against a table, then propelled himself forward like a catapult.

York stopped him with a solid jolt in the chest before he could even deliver a blow. Flash appeared utterly confused by Dan's blow. Apparently, his strength and weight had overpowered everyone he had fought before. Neither was having any effect on Dan York.

Flash made another attempt, getting through York's guard for a glancing blow on his ear. York ignored it and waded in, sending Flash reeling backward again. Flash missed the table this time and staggered halfway to the door.

When he stopped, he shot one glance around the room at the surprised faces of the spectators.

'Take him, Flash,' one man said and gave him a shove toward York.

Flash took one step, then stopped suddenly, his hand diving for his gun. York had seen a move like that before. Once in a little

10

town in Texas a few days north of Fort Griffin, Dan had been almost too slow in reacting to it.

His response now equaled Flash's move. But there the equality ended. York's speed was as overpowering as his physical strength had been. Flash was beginning to fall when his first and only shot plowed into the floor an inch from the toe of York's boot.

The echo of the two shots faded into a sudden deathly silence. Nothing moved in the room except the eyes of the spectators, flipping from the body on the floor to the towering newcomer who stood quietly watching for signs that someone else might take up the battle. Only disbelieving stares met Dan's eyes.

Finally, one man said softly to nobody in particular, 'Flash was the fastest gun in four counties.'

The silence broken, another man spoke up. 'Best brawler, too.'

'He ain't neither one now,' the bartender said. He stared at York and shook his head. 'Never thought I'd see the day when Flash would be whipped with either fists or guns.'

York turned to leave. The awe in the men in the room might suddenly turn to mob violence to avenge the fall of their hero.

'Are you any relation to Tom York who was killed in the accident up in the Trap?' the bartender asked as York reached the door.

Dan turned his head. 'He was my father.'

Just then a man slamming through the batwings almost collided with Dan York. Dan saw the star on his chest.

The sheriff stopped, his eyes flashing over the room. 'What's going on? Who killed him?' He pointed at the body on the floor.

'He did,' the bartender said, nodding toward Dan. 'Says his name is Dan York. He's mighty good with his fists and just as good with a gun. York, this is Hector Posey, the sheriff here in Goldtown.'

'I'll have to arrest you, York,' Posey said.

'It was a fair fight,' York protested.

'I ain't saying it wasn't,' the sheriff said. 'But till it's proved that way, you'll have to sit it out in the jail. We're going to stop the killing in this county.'

York had always obeyed the law. He followed his first impulse now and let the sheriff take his gun, then walked ahead of him out to the street. He moved up the street in the direction the lawman pointed.

Glancing back, Dan saw that the crowd inside the saloon had followed him and the sheriff to the swinging doors and stopped there. Either they felt that the sheriff had everything in hand or they still hadn't overcome the awe that had gripped them at seeing their champion handled so easily.

Dan considered his situation. Already he was wishing he hadn't let the sheriff take his

12

gun. Those awestruck men back there could quickly become a mob. He had only wanted to get an answer to a simple question. It hadn't been as simple as he had expected. But then nothing had been simple lately.

A short time before, York had arrived in Dodge City at the end of a trail drive and word reached him that his father and step-mother had been killed in an accident in Nugget Canyon, Colorado. York had drawn the money he'd earned on the drive and headed for Denver to settle his father's business.

Tom York had made out a will and Dan learned to his surprise that his father and stepmother had much more property than he had imagined.

With the estate settled, he had taken the job of delivering the cash and the deed to the property that had been left to his stepsister, Carlita Frake. He had volunteered for the job because he wanted to come here and investigate that accident anyway.

The lawyer seemed greatly relieved to let Dan have the job of making the delivery to Carlita Frake.

Dan had had time because no other job was calling him after he'd delivered that herd to Dodge City.

Sitting in the Goldtown jail, however, did not fit into his plans. At the front of the jail he stopped.

'How long do you figure on keeping me locked up?' he demanded.

'Just till we can hold a hearing,' Posey said. 'Judge Wagasy is in town. He can hold the hearing in the morning.'

'Will anyone tell the truth?' Dan asked.

'Just being a stranger ain't going to work against you,' the sheriff said.

York wasn't sure whether to believe him or not. But if he'd been going to argue the point, he should have done it back in the saloon. He moved across the sheriff's office and into a cell. Then the lawman slammed the door and turned the key.

The sheriff left and York had time to contemplate his situation. He had foreseen no trouble on this trip until after he'd delivered Carlita's inheritance. If he found evidence of foul play in the deaths of Tom and Renetta York, then he might have trouble as he closed in on the culprits. But as far as he could see, what had happened had no connection with the accident that had killed Tom York. Flash had been ready to fight before he found out that Dan's name was York.

York slept well considering his impatience to get out of his cell. Sheriff Posey brought his breakfast at six o'clock, then came back for him a few minutes before eight.

Heck Posey was a short man, too heavy for his height. He looked small standing beside Dan York. They left the jail and moved over

14

to the small courthouse that stood next door. There were a half dozen tiny offices in one half of the building. The other half was the courtroom. It was crowded when Posey led his prisoner inside.

The judge was at a desk on a low platform at one end of the room. He was only a little taller than the sheriff and perhaps a little heavier. Not used to a lot of hard labor, York decided. His face had a ruddy complexion, but his muddy brown eyes had a sharpness that belied his cherubic appearance.

The judge rapped a gavel on the desk. 'Sheriff, you tell me what you know about the case.'

That took only a minute since the sheriff had arrived after the shooting was over.

The judge pointed a finger at the bartender then. 'Al, tell me what you saw.'

'This big fellow came in and asked where Sam Frake's ranch was and I told him,' the bartender said. 'When he started to leave, Flash picked a fight. Flash had never seen the man he couldn't lick. But he sure saw him yesterday. Then when Flash went for his gun, he was a dead man before he could draw another breath.'

'Self-defense?' Judge Wagasy asked.

'Don't like to go against our own people,' the bartender said. 'But it sure wasn't this fellow's idea to start shooting.'

Two other men who had been in the saloon

the day before were called out of the crowd by the judge. Both verified the bartender's story. York was amazed.

'Got to call it self-defense then,' the judge ruled.

A yell came from the back of the room. 'You can't do that. You let him go and this town will be burned to the ground.'

'Just hold your horses,' Wagasy said. 'It's self-defense and that's that. But there is one other charge against the defendant, carrying a gun within the city limits of Goldtown. For that offense, I fine you, Dan York, one thousand dollars.'

Dan leaped forward as if he'd been prodded by an angry bull. 'What?' he roared. 'There was no sign saying a man couldn't carry a gun. And how about Flash? He sure had a gun.'

'Calm down,' Wagasy ordered. 'Heck, you keep a tight rein on him.'

The sheriff nodded and took a firm grip on York's arm.

York jerked loose and faced the judge again. 'I can't dig up a thousand dollars,' he roared. 'What about Flash's gun?'

'Can't fine a dead man,' Wagasy said. 'I'll give you two alternatives if you can't pay the fine.'

York made a fast calculation. He had paid his widowed sister, Elizabeth, most of the cash he'd inherited for her share of the little

16

ranch that was in the estate. He still had Carlita's share of the money with him, but he was not going to use that to pay his fine. In fact, he wasn't going to let anyone know he had that money.

'What are the choices?' Dan asked grimly.

'Six months in jail at hard labor. Or you can take the body of the man you killed back to his family.'

York's suspicions flared. That last choice was too simple, too easy. Someone in the crowd yelled his approval of the sentence. That added to Dan's suspicions. He glared at the judge and took his time reaching a decision.

If he was going to investigate the accident that had killed his father and stepmother, he couldn't allow himself to be locked up in jail for six months, especially considering the slave labor that went with that sentence. Taking the body of the dead man home would be the quickest way to appease this judge. He knew it wouldn't be simple or safe. But it seemed the only thing to do.

'Why do you want me to take the dead man home?' Dan asked suspiciously, watching the judge's expression.

Wagasy kept a poker face. 'So neither the sheriff nor I will have to do it. I've given you three choices. That's two more than most prisoners get. What will it be?'

'You know the answer to that,' York said. 'I

17

can't pay the fine and I won't be a slave for you. I'll take the body home.'

A unified sigh ran over the watching crowd. Even the judge let his face relax. But it was the sheriff, Heck Posey, who showed the most satisfaction, or maybe it was relief.

'You'll start within the hour,' Judge Wagasy said. 'You'll be given a team and wagon and you can tie your horse behind. Just leave the wagon at the ranch after you've made the delivery.'

York's suspicions were still growing. 'Where do I take this body?'

'To Sam Frake's Box F ranch,' Wagasy said. 'The man you killed was Jeff Frake, Sam's only son.'

'You're a dead man the minute Sam sees you,' a man just a few feet from York said.

CHAPTER TWO

Dan struggled to collect his thoughts. The man they called Flash had been Jeff Frake, Sam Frake's son. He'd heard tales of Sam Frake and his domination of the valley where he lived. He'd heard of his terrifying temper. Apparently, what he'd heard had not been an exaggeration. These people were in awe of him.

Maybe it was Sam Frake's reputation that had propelled Jeff Frake into the position he had enjoyed here in Goldtown. Flash obviously hadn't been the fighter or the gunman people had given him credit for being. Perhaps they knew that if they fought Jeff Frake, even if they were successful, they'd pay for it when Sam Frake got to them.

Jeff had been Carlita Frake's blood cousin. Maybe she was also his sister by adoption; she carried the Frake name. She probably thought of him as a brother. Dan had never seen Carlita Frake, but he was soon going to meet her. More important, he was going to see Sam Frake and tell him that he'd killed his son.

Judge Edward Wagasy adjourned court while Dan was assessing the situation. Now he was faced with carrying out the judge's sentence. The thought crossed his mind that if everybody was afraid to face Sam Frake, no one was going to make sure that he, Dan, took the body to the Box F and handed it over to Frake.

He would do it, anyway. York couldn't remember seeing anyone or anything that he was afraid of. Sam Frake might be the first. He certainly wasn't anticipating a confrontation, especially in view of the business he had to conduct with Carlita.

The sheriff took York's arm and escorted him to the door. Obviously, he was going to take no chances that York would disappear the minute he was out of the courtroom.

Outside, Sheriff Posey dispatched a man to get a team and wagon from the livery barn just across the street from the courthouse. While they waited, a redheaded young woman with sparkling blue eyes came bouncing out of the courthouse and approached York, ignoring the sheriff.

Her eyes ran over Dan from his Stetson to his worn boots. 'You're no miner, are you?' she said bluntly.

York shook his head. 'Not anymore. Just finished a cattle drive from Texas not long ago.'

'You're sure a big man,' she said, her lips parting in a smile that revealed gleaming teeth. 'I like big men.'

York shrugged. 'My pa was a big man.'

'Aren't you afraid to take Flash back to his father?'

'I'm not looking forward to it,' Dan said. 'But I'm not as afraid of Sam Frake as I am of spending six months in jail.'

Her smile stayed on her lips. 'I think you're a brave man. I like brave men.'

He'd anticipated that last remark. The girl was a flirt and this obviously was her approach. He had to admit she was the prettiest flirt he'd run into recently.

'I'm Winnie Wagasy,' she said.

She turned to another woman who had just come out of the courthouse. The second woman was a little taller and a little heavier and twenty years older but otherwise a carbon copy of Winnie.

'This is my mother, Gilda Wagasy,' the girl said.

'The judge's wife?' York asked, acknowledging the introduction.

Gilda Wagasy nodded. 'Come along, Winnie. This man has more to do than chatter with us.'

York watched them go up the street, Winnie turning to flash another smile at him before they disappeared.

'A little young to be the judge's wife, isn't she?' Dan said to the sheriff.

'Gilda?' Sheriff Posey said. 'She's about twenty years younger than the judge. She's

21

been the belle of Goldtown for a long time, but now Winnie's getting big enough to take over. You've got more important things to think about than Gilda and Winnie Wagasy.'

'I reckon,' York admitted. 'What will Sam Frake do when I get there?'

'Nobody knows for sure what Sam's going to do. That's one thing that makes him so dangerous. Jeff was his only son. He has one daughter about four years younger than Jeff, but it was Jeff he put his store in. Here.' He took York's gun from under his belt and handed it to him.

'You must expect Frake to go after me as soon as I show up,' Dan said, sliding the gun into his holster.

'He'll go after whoever takes his son back to him in a wooden box,' Posey said. 'I'm guessing he won't ask questions till he's killed somebody.'

York nodded. He understood now why Sheriff Posey had looked so relieved when York had said he'd take the body home. Otherwise, the job would likely have fallen to Posey. Even though he'd had nothing to do with the death of Jeff Frake, Posey obviously thought that Sam Frake would murder him just to strike out at the human race for killing his son.

York wondered how any man could instill that kind of fear in people who were not even his close neighbors. Sam Frake lived up in the valley around Nugget, not down here near Goldtown. But there was little doubt that Sam Frake was feared and dreaded by everyone who knew him. Dan didn't know him and maybe that was why he wasn't petrified at the thought of facing him.

'You're not giving me much chance of living through this,' York said.

'You figure your own chances,' Posey said. 'Even if you handle Sam Frake, which nobody around here can, he has two hired hands that are liable to be there. One is a big fellow, Fred Cluff. He was Jeff's best friend. He'll be almost as wild as Sam when he finds out Jeff's dead. The other is a cousin of Jeff's, Lennie Swift. Lennie is the son of Sam's sister. A little weasel of a man who'd do anything to please Sam. Figure your odds against that stacked deck.'

'Why didn't the judge just sentence me to hang?'

'Let me tell you, you didn't lose any friends in Goldtown by getting rid of Jeff Frake,' Posey said. 'The judge might have turned you loose, but if he hadn't, we'd all have had to account to Sam. There's always the slim chance that you'll get away from the Box F. After all, you did show up Flash pretty bad, Al tells me.'

York nodded. Judge Wagasy had given the whole town a way out. They were saving

23

their own hides by throwing him to the wolf. He supposed he couldn't blame them, but it rankled him that he was the goat for all the weak-kneed inhabitants of Goldtown.

'Do you know Carlita?' Dan asked.

Posey said, 'Sam's daughter? A real pretty girl. Doesn't look anything like the rest of the family. We don't see her often. She comes down to Goldtown once in a while with her folks now that all the stores in Nugget have closed.'

A team and wagon rumbled away from the livery barn and down to the hardware store nearby. York guessed the town's mortician, if it had one, worked in the back of the hardware store.

'I've heard people mention a trap up in Nugget Canyon. What are they talking about?'

The sheriff took his eyes from the wagon and glanced at Dan. 'It's a place in the canyon about halfway between here and Nugget. A creek runs along the canyon. That canyon is extremely narrow at the Trap. There's a good-sized waterfall in the creek and the road is very steep as it climbs past those falls. There's a sharp drop-off to the rocks below along the side of the creek. That's the Trap. Several horses and six people have wandered too close to that drop-off and fallen over.'

York frowned. 'Were the people drunk?'

'Some of them may have been. But I don't figure this last couple who went over were drunk.'

'Tell me about them.'

Posey started to speak, then stopped and stared at Dan. 'It was a man named York and his wife. Your name is York. Any relation?'

'He was my father,' Dan said.

'Was that why you killed Jeff Frake?' Posey asked after sorting out his thoughts. 'Do you think he had something to do with it?'

York shook his head. 'I didn't know who he was till this morning. And he was on the prod before he found out who I was.' Dan studied the sheriff's face. 'What do you know about that wreck?'

Posey shrugged. 'It was an accident, pure and simple. The team just drifted too close to the edge and went over, according to the tracks.'

York somehow doubted that, but he didn't say anything. He had never known a horse to wander over a cliff even on the darkest night unless something forced him to. Dan intended to find out exactly what had happened.

The wagon came from the hardware store with a long box in the back. York's horse was tied to the endgate. The driver pulled up in front of the courthouse and jumped down, handing the reins to the sheriff. Posey motioned Dan onto the seat.

25

'I don't question the fact that you acted in self-defence when you shot Jeff Frake,' the older man said, looking up at York on the high seat. 'But Sam Frake ain't going to think about that. I reckon it's a harsh sentence to make you take Jeff back to the Box F, but somebody has to. I wish you luck.'

York clucked to the team and started up the street. Three men with rifles mounted horses and rode along well behind the wagon. Just making sure he went up the canyon, York thought. He guessed he couldn't blame them for suspecting he might not follow through with the orders.

The riders made no attempt to catch up with York but stayed within rifle range of him. He had no chance to turn off the road. Less than a mile from town, the road entered the lower end of Nugget Canyon. After that, there was only one way to go, and that was up the canyon.

Dan looked back after a short distance and saw that the riders were still following but even farther back now. He surmised that there was no way to get off this road until he was up in the valley of Sam Frake's ranch.

He let his mind go back to the sheriff. Posey seemed like a decent man. Afraid of Sam Frake, perhaps, but it seemed that everybody in Goldtown was afraid of him. York wished he had pressed Posey for every detail he knew about the accident that had

26

killed Tom and Renetta York. An impulse told him it was no accident, and Dan usually followed his impulses.

Dan remembered what his mother had said about his impulsiveness and explosive temper. She had died in 1866, just a year after Tom York had brought his family to Colorado where he and his son had worked in the mines. Dan York had been in many brawls. Although he usually came out on top, it kept him in trouble much of the time.

York's mother had compared Dan's disposition to a wild wind. His impulses carried him one way and his temper often shot him off in a different direction. He'd have to be a big man, she said, to ride that wild wind. If he wasn't he'd come to a sudden end.

More than once in the years since he'd left the mines to drive a freight wagon and later drive cattle, he had thought he'd come to that sudden end. Each time it had been the result of either his temper or some sudden impulse that he'd followed.

Ahead Dan saw the waterfall Sheriff Posey had said was in the canyon. The road climbed sharply above the falls. The road was narrow, little more than a ledge clinging to the cliff. Before it reached the level of the creek above the falls, it was fifty or more feet above the rocks at the foot of the falls. Anybody going over the edge here would be battered to death on those rocks. It was easy to understand why they called this the Trap.

There was no way to turn around, and you had to be very careful when going up or down. Dan's eyes darted ahead and to either side. If someone wanted to get rid of him right now, all he'd need to do would be to make a sudden appearance or sound that would startle the horses. If they dodged toward the edge of the road, they'd go over. He could see the wreckage of a buggy down there on the rocks.

It could have been some animal that had startled Tom York's team, but it could also have been some person. Dan was going to believe it was the latter until he could prove that it wasn't. He couldn't stop now, but he'd come back later and examine this place carefully. For his father was too careful to have an accident.

Once even with the creek, the road widened and leveled out. The narrow canyon stretched a couple of miles farther before York entered another hemmed-in valley similar to the one around Goldtown, only smaller.

The valley tilted from the northwest to the Southeast and the creek skipped noisily across that tilt, fed by springs and melting snow in the mountains.

Just a short distance above the entrance to the canyon, a small town nestled on the right bank of the creek. Far to the left, up near the mountains, York could see some ranch buildings. That would be the Box F. It was the only ranch in this valley, from what he'd heard.

Reining the team toward the town, he pulled into the one long street. The place was silent, as dead as last year's weed stalks that grew in the corral behind the livery barn, the first building he came to. Ahead he saw a saloon and some stores on either side of the street. A church was nearby on his right. A dozen houses or so were situated farther up the street. To the east side of town stood a big two-story house, a mansion compared to the other houses. A short distance separated it from the other nearby buildings.

York had heard that Nugget was a ghost town, but he expected to find someone here. His wagon creaked and clattered over the ruts in the road as he moved along. He saw a second road angling across the creek, apparently leading toward the ranch. He'd follow that.

Before he'd gone much beyond the livery barn, though, a man limped out from a house well behind the barn. York pulled the team to a stop and waited. The man was small with a peg for a foot on is right leg. His dark skin, black hair, and dark eyes suggested Mexican blood.

'You lost, stranger?' the man asked with a slight Mexican accent.

York shook his head. 'I'm heading for the Box F. I've got Jeff Frake's body in the wagon.'

The man whistled softly. 'If I was you, I'd think twice before I headed into the Box F with that load. Sam Frake will go wild. He might even think you killed Jeff. You'll be dead before you can tell him different.'

'I did kill him,' Dan said. 'That's why I've been given the job of taking his body home.'

The man nodded. 'That's one way of sentencing you to death. Easier than hanging.' He limped up to the front of the wagon. 'I'm Joe Vicarona. People call me Joe. You did the country a favor by killing Jeff Frake. Now let me do you a favor. I'll take him to the ranch. Old Sam might listen to me before he starts shooting. He'll know I didn't kill him. He won't listen to you, especially if you're crazy enough to admit you killed Jeff.'

'It was a fair fight,' Dan said.

'Nothing's fair to Sam Frake unless he comes out ahead,' Vicarona said.

York heard a sound to his right and turned to see a tall white-headed man with a neatly trimmed mustache come past one of the stores. He had probably come from that mansion York had seen as he drove into town.

'My neighbor, Horace Trillingham,' Vicarona said. 'Only neighbor I got left here. He's an Englishman who made it big mining here and just stayed when everybody else left.'

York watched the proud walk of the tall man as he approached the wagon. Joe Vicarona introduced them and explained York's mission.

'I say you'd be a foolish man to take that burden to Mr Frake,' Trillingham said after the three had chatted a while. 'He can be rather nasty at times.'

'I told him we'd take the wagon up there,' Vicarona said. He looked at Dan. 'Sam Frake lets Horace and me live here to keep up the looks of the place. Sam owns this entire valley now, even this town.'

'That wouldn't keep him from killing you if he's as vicious as you say he is,' Dan said.

'He'll know we didn't do it,' Vicarona said. 'If we had, we wouldn't be fool enough to bring back the remains.'

'Do you know Carlita Frake?' Dan asked.

'Ah,' Trillingham sighed, his eyes lighting up. 'The apple of my eye!'

'Don't claim her just for yourself, you old goat,' Vicarona said. 'She means just as much to me as to you.'

York looked from one man to the other. Both their faces reflected a joy that was obviously caused by the mention of Carlita's name. He guessed the two men thought a great deal of each other, too.

'I take it you see her often,' Dan guessed.

'She comes down here almost every day,' Vicarona said. 'Brings us nice things to eat.

31

Claims we don't know how to cook right for ourselves.'

'Hard to understand how such a sweet thing can belong to a man like Mr Frake,' Trillingham added.

Dan looked across the creek toward the ranch. 'I'd better get my chore done.' He clucked to the team.

'I wouldn't advise it,' Trillingham shouted after him.

York wasn't advising it for himself, either, but this was his mission. Besides, Carlita was up there. A third of the money that the store and home of Tom and Renetta York had brought at the sale was Carlita's share. Carlita had also inherited a half interest in the little ranch in the foothills. Apparently, Renetta had inherited that ranch from her second husband. Dan had inherited a fourth interest and he had bought his sister's fourth interest. Today he'd deliver Carlita's money and tell her about her half interest in the ranch.

It didn't take the wagon long to cross the distance to the ranch. The three riflemen had followed as far as Nugget and stopped, apparently convinced that Dan was going to carry out his mission.

York's approach was noticed by the people at the Box F. Dan saw two men come from the barn to join the man and two women who had come out on the porch of the

32

house. They had all moved out to the yard by the time he reached them. Obviously, the Box F didn't receive many visitors.

Dan quickly picked out Sam Frake. He was even bigger than Jeff Frake and the two shared the same features except that the father's eyes were midnight black instead of brown. A sense of power radiated from him. He stepped out ahead of the others like a stallion ready to meet a challenge.

Dan quickly flashed his eyes over the others in the yard. To one side of Frake was a woman about his age, perhaps forty-five. She looked small compared to him, but she was average in size. She had blue eyes and auburn hair in sharp contrast to the black-haired, black-eyed girl beside her.

The girl was an inch or two taller than the woman and at least thirty pounds lighter. Dan guessed her to be no more than twenty. Her hair was combed straight back from her forehead and done up in a bun on the back of her head, but he could imagine how beautiful it would be if it were allowed to stream down her back. Her skin was an olive tan and her lips were a lovely red. York let his breath out slowly. He had never seen such a pretty young woman in all his travels.

He shot his eyes across to the other side of Frake. The two men there were a sharp contrast. The redheaded one with light blue eyes would have been a big man anywhere except standing beside Sam Frake. The other man was small and as colorless as a desert dune, his hair sandy, his eyes gray. His cheeks were sallow in spite of work that surely kept him outside a great deal. The prominent feature that York noticed was the long hooked nose. On his small face, that stood out like a lighthouse on a beach.

'What brings you here?' Frake demanded gruffly.

York stood up in the wagon. 'I stopped in Goldtown yesterday,' he said. 'A young man there picked a fight with me. I shot him.'

The significance to Dan's words hit Mrs Frake, but Sam Frake only glared at him.

'What's that to us?' he demanded.

'They told me his name was Jeff Frake. I've got his body here.'

Sam Frake's face twisted as if a mule had kicked him in the stomach. The next instance, his hand shot to his gun like lightning.

CHAPTER THREE

Dan York had anticipated Sam Frake's sudden grab for his gun. At the first move the rancher made, York's hand snapped up his .45. It was aimed at Frake before Frake's gun had completely cleared leather.

The rancher's move halted as quickly as it had begun and he slowly let his gun slip back into the holster. His eyes bored into York's, and there was no surrender in them even though he had backed off from the challenge.

'A gunslick!' Frake muttered. 'Who hired you to kill my boy?'

'Nobody,' York said. 'I wasn't looking for trouble, but your son was. I whipped him with my fists, but he wouldn't settle for that. He tried for his gun.'

'How many mothers' sons have you killed that way?' Frake asked, his voice breaking in fury.

'None that wasn't trying to kill me,' Dan said.

York had been concentrating on Sam Frake. A moment's slackening of his own guard and Frake would try again for his gun. Now Dan caught a movement to his left. He

35

shot a glance that way. The little man was gliding over to get out of York's vision.

With a bare flip of the gun muzzle, Dan stopped him. 'Get over close to the others and stay there,' he snapped.

The little man moved back with alacrity to stand in the shadow of the two big men. York again concentrated on Frake. There was a wildness in the rancher's eyes that showed he might do anything.

Tears were streaming down the woman's face and she stared silently at the wagon as if she couldn't believe what York had said. There were tears in the girl's eyes, too, and she was just as silent as the woman. York felt sorry for them. He would feel sympathy for the man, too, if he would allow it, but Sam Frake was not looking for sympathy. He wanted revenge.

'It was ruled self-defense by the judge,' Dan said calmly. 'My only punishment was to bring the body back home. I've done that now. I'll leave the team and wagon here. I guess somebody from Goldtown will pick them up.'

'You ain't just riding away after killing my boy,' Frake said. 'You'll have to kill every one of us here before you do that.'

Dan centered his gun on Frake. 'Nobody needs to die. But if anybody does, you'll be the first.'

Mrs Frake pleaded. 'Mister, won't you

please go? One of my men dead is enough.'

'I couldn't agree more,' Dan said, but he didn't take his eyes off Frake.

'If you go now, I'll hunt you down like a skunk,' Sam Frake said, breathing hard. 'Put that gun away and we'll have a go at it right now.'

'You had your go,' Dan said. 'You know how it came out. Drop your gun belt.'

'I don't take off my gun for nobody,' Frake snapped.

'You're going to take it off now,' Dan said. 'Or you'll be sorry. I won't kill you, but I'll fix you so you won't be drawing a gun for the rest of your life.'

That got through to Frake. Dan saw his eyes flicker for the first time. He wasn't afraid of dying, but he didn't want to live with no chance to get revenge. That evidently decided him.

'Before you see many more sunrises, I'll find you again,' Frake muttered as he slowly unbuckled his gun belt and let it fall.

York's gun shifted slightly to cover the two hired hands. 'Off with your hardware, too,' he said.

The defiance in the eyes of the bigger man had faded when he saw Sam Frake shed his gun. Both men dropped their gun belts.

'Now back away,' York commanded and the men stepped back.

Dan stepped down to the hub of the front

wheel, then to the ground, keeping his eyes on the men. Backing to his horse tied to the endgate, he flipped the reins loose. He had to take his eyes off the men for just an instant to get his hand on the cinch and tighten it.

He thought Frake might make a try for his gun on the ground in front of him, but he didn't. When he'd taken off his gun, he apparently had decided to wait for a better time. There was no doubt in York's mind that the rancher would try again. He'd keep trying till he succeeded or died.

With the cinch tight, Dan swung into the saddle. No one had moved. Kicking his horse into a gallop, he thundered out of the yard back toward Nugget. He heard yells and curses behind him and a gun popped twice, but Dan was already out of six-gun range.

At Nugget, he stopped short of the first buildings and looked back. He half expected to see the three men in hot pursuit, but he saw no one. Turning, he rode slowly into town. Joe Vicarona and Horace Trillingham had apparently been watching his retreat from the Box F. They met him with smiles.

'Didn't think you'd get off the Box F alive,' Vicarona said.

'I didn't exactly get a warm welcome,' York said.

'Was Sam alone?' Trillingham asked.

'There were three men and two women there.'

Trillingham whistled. 'The whole outfit.'

'The big hired hand would have been Fred Cluff and the little one Lennie Swift,' Vicarona said. 'It's a wonder Cluff didn't team up with Sam to get you.'

'Frake thought he could do it himself,' Dan said. 'What about the girl, Carlita? Is there any way I can get to talk to her alone?'

'What do you want with her?' Vicarona asked suspiciously.

'I've got something to give her,' Dan said, feeling he could trust these two men.

'Any value to it?'

'It's money,' York said. 'Quite a bit of it.'

'Then don't give it to her now,' Vicarona warned. 'Sam Frake will get it.'

'Why?' Dan asked.

'Because he handles every penny on the Box F and doles it out as he sees fit,' Trillingham put in. 'If you give Carlita any money, he'll take it away from her. And he'll probably keep it for himself.'

'Did Sam treat his boy this way, too?'

'No,' Trillingham said. 'It's a bloody shame the way he treats Carlita compared to Jeff. He won't let Carlita have anything, not even a new dress. But he gave Jeff everything he wanted. Never made him work.'

'Did you know she's adopted?' Dan asked.

Trillingham just stared at York, but Vicarona nodded. 'I did,' he said. 'The Frakes claim her as their own and Carlita may think she really is.'

'I made this trip to give her this inheritance from her mother's estate,' York said. 'What would you suggest I do about it?'

'Hang on to it until you can get Carlita away from Frake,' Trillingham suggested.

'Just how am I to do that? Even if I got her away from Frake, she might go back. Wouldn't he take it then?'

'He sure would,' Vicarona said. 'What Horace means is for you to wait till Carlita leaves home, then give it to her.'

'Any chance she'll do that soon?'

'I reckon she will when she marries Omar Perkins,' Trillingham said.

'Who is Omar Perkins?'

'He's the son of the banker in Goldtown,' Vicarona said. 'He stands to own that bank one of these days. His pa ain't in very good shape. Omar is practically running the bank now. It should be a good marriage for Carlita.'

Dan was getting the feeling that these two old men were more concerned about the welfare of Carlita Frake than their own. Maybe that wasn't so strange. They were surely lonely men, living here in this ghost town. If Carlita came down almost every day and brought them things to eat, it was natural for them to think the sun rose and set in her.

40

'He's the only young man old Sam will let her see,' Trillingham said, anger in his voice. 'I don't know how he figures on managing it, but I think he plans to run that bank himself one of these days.'

'Horace is probably right,' Vicarona said. 'Sam sees something to gain from this or he wouldn't let Carlita see young Perkins.'

'Maybe he needs money and thinks he can borrow from Perkins if Perkins is his son-in-law,' Dan suggested.

'Could be something like that,' Vicarona said. 'He was getting rich when he could sell his beef to people in Nugget. It was a good market and they bought it even if the price was high. But now that Nugget is gone, Sam will have to sell down at Goldtown. Trouble is, Burr Belling has that market cornered for his beef, and he ain't about to let Sam horn in on it.'

'Why doesn't Frake just sell his land and go down where there is an open market?' Dan asked. 'He can sell his cattle and start a new ranch somewhere.'

'You don't know Burr Belling,' Trillingham said. 'He wants Sam's valley and his herd. He won't pay a fair price, and he won't let Frake take his cattle out.'

'There's only one way in or out of this valley,' Vicarona added. 'That's down Nugget Canyon past the Trap. Try taking a herd of cattle down that narrow ledge when somebody down there don't want you to.'

York understood. If Frake couldn't get his herd out and he was unwilling to sell at Belling's price, he was facing a real impasse.

'I'd say there's a bloody war brewing between Sam Frake and Belling,' Trillingham said.

'I hear there's been several accidents at he Trap,' York said. 'Do you know anything about the buggy that went over the edge about a month ago?'

'I heard about it,' Trillingham said. 'It's not the first accident that has happened there. I'm surprised there aren't more accidents.'

'I figure the team got spooked by some wild animal or something,' Vicarona said. 'Wouldn't take much to send them over the edge.'

That was too simple an explanation for Dan. He didn't doubt that these two men believed that. But he wouldn't accept it until he'd investigated it thoroughly. To do that, he'd have to stay there a while. Anyway, he had to give Carlita her inheritance.

'I think I'll stick around and see if I can get to talk to Carlita before I go back to Denver,' he said.

'That ain't very smart, with Sam Frake after your hide like a starving coyote after a rabbit,' Vicarona said. 'But if you want to stay, just pick out a house and move in. There are plenty of empty houses in town, and we try to keep them all in fair shape.'

Dan led his horse down the alley past a store toward the creek. He had seen a small house there that looked cozy. There was a small barn not far away, and he put his horse there. There was even some hay in the lean-to behind the barn. He fed the horse, then carried his bedroll into the house.

It was a small house, but it still contained a stove and a broken table. Dan also found a section of tree trunk that obviously had been used as a chair. There was even an old set of bed springs and he spread his bedroll on that. Within minutes, he was comfortably settled in his new lodgings.

Dawn found Dan York eating his breakfast, and he was soon on his way out of town toward the Trap. The empty houses stared at him like the unseeing eyes of a dead monster. Trillingham and Vicarona apparently weren't up when Dan rode out. It was just as well. He didn't feel like explaining why he was determined to examine the wreck below the Trap. They were convinced it had been an accident; he wasn't.

The canyon swallowed Dan and the town disappeared behind him. As the red-streaked gray walls closed in on him, squeezing together like the jaws of a nutcracker, York felt a chill running over him. There was a sense of foreboding in the canyon walls, like the silent threat of the calm before a storm.

The creek beside the road gained speed as it tumbled toward the falls. Then the walls really squeezed together, bringing the creek and the road into a narrow passage. The road yielded half its width to the rushing water and suddenly both turned sharply downward.

The falls plunged almost fifty feet into a frothing pool while the road slanted down at a precarious angle as if frantic to reach the same level as the creek. York held his horse to a slow pace as he studied the canyon.

Below the falls, just past the pool, was the area that fascinated York. He looked down at the wreckage of the buggy on the rocks.

Dan imagined a buggy coming to meet him now. If he spurred his horse toward the buggy, perhaps waving his hat, the wagon team would almost certainly lunge to get out of his way. One misstep and the horses would plunge over the edge of the road, dragging the buggy with them.

Even if the team simply backed up, the buggy would likely go over, dragging the horses behind it. An undisturbed team, however, would never step off that ledge. His team yesterday hadn't come close to disaster heading up this grade.

Dan rode on to the bottom of the steep grade, then turned off the road and headed for the foot of the falls. Dismounting near the wreck of the buggy, he walked slowly

around it. He wasn't sure what he was looking for, but his instincts told him to look.

Two of the buggy wheels were off to one
side. The impact of the fall had thrown them
from the axles. One wheel was broken near
the buggy and the other turned under the
wreck. The bed of the buggy was smashed
into splinters but not scattered as Dan had
expected. Gingerly he lifted some pieces of
the buggy. He didn't really expect to find
any clues as to what had happened any
more than he had up on the road. It had
been more than a month since the wreck. If
Tom and Renetta had any baggage with
them, it had been taken away by someone.

Dan did see a shoe under the wreck,
apparently one of his father's. The force of
the crash must have knocked it off his foot,
and the men removing the bodies hadn't
stopped to look for it. While examining the
bed of the buggy, Dan saw a paper sticking
out from under a broken piece of wood. He
lifted the wood and took it out.

It was a rain-soaked letter. York studied
the envelope. The address was smeared by
water stains, but he could still read it. It was
addressed to Mrs Thomas York. And it had
been sent by Mrs Samuel Frake.

Eagerly Dan took out the letter. It hadn't
been damaged as much by the rain as the
envelope had been. He felt a pang of guilt at
reading the letter from Genevieve Frake to

her sister, Renetta York, but he had come here to pry.

The handwriting was clear, although smeared in places where water had soaked through the envelope. Dan's eyes scanned the first part of the letter, which was only news of simple people in an isolated valley. York could almost feel the loneliness radiating from the page. Then a paragraph caught his eye and made his blood race.

'Carlita is going to Goldtown tonight to a dance. I will send this letter with her to mail. I'm not sure that Sam always mails the letters I give him. Now that there is no longer a post office in Nugget, all letters have to be taken to Goldtown. I'm sure you have written to me more often than I have received your letters. I wish you would come and visit me. I know it won't be pleasant for you, but I want you to see Carlita. She is a beautiful young lady. I have tried to raise her right. But there isn't any way she can learn refinement here like she ought to know. If you come, be careful. Sam doesn't want Carlita to see you. He has forbidden me to talk to her about you. I think you have a right to see her, and she has a right to know you.'

There was more to the letter, but none of it interested Dan. Carefully he folded the paper and slid it back into the envelope, then put it in his pocket.

Mounting his horse again, he headed on

toward Goldtown, his mind on that letter. Was that the key to the wreck? What little Dan had seen of Sam Frake told him that Frake would do whatever was necessary to get what he wanted. According to the letter, he definitely didn't want Renetta York to see Carlita. Would he kill Renetta to make sure she didn't get to the Box F? Dan thought that he might, even if it meant killing Renetta's husband as well. And if Sam Frake had killed Dan's father and stepmother, he would pay for it.

CHAPTER FOUR

Dan was deep in thought when his horse carried him out of the canyon into the wide valley that held Goldtown. The town was on the northeast side of Nugget Creek. To the west of the creek was a wide valley ringed with mountains. York again saw the ranch he'd noticed on his arrival in this area. It looked more prosperous than Frake's Box F up in the valley above the falls.

Dan was still thinking about the two ranches when he reached the jail. He stopped and went in to see the sheriff. The office in front of the jail was empty.

Going back to his horse, Dan studied the town, looking at the various stores and other buildings. He decided there was a good chance that the sheriff was at the saloon. Leaving his horse behind, he headed for the Lucky Strike.

Stepping into the dim interior, Dan saw Posey lounging against the bar talking to the bartender. Both men looked up when he came in, their eyes popping.

'Didn't expect to see you walk in,' the bartender said.

'Did you take Jeff's body to the Box F?'

Sheriff Posey asked.

York nodded. 'You warned me what to expect, so I was ready. Sam Frake has every appearance of being a fire-eater, but he didn't seem to have any appetite for fire mixed with lead.'

The bartender ran his eyes over Dan with new respect. 'You mean you told him you killed Flash?'

'I told him exactly what happened,' Dan said. 'Then I hid behind my gun till I got away from there.' He paused, watching the two men closely. 'What do you know about the wreck up near the falls? I saw the busted buggy as I was going past.'

'An accident,' the bartender said quickly. 'Horses got spooked.'

'Did you see the people who were killed in that wreck?'

The sheriff answered. 'Sure, we saw them. Seemed like decent people. Can't figure why them or anybody else would go to visit the Frakes.'

'I remember they ordered lemonade here,' the bartender added. 'Wasn't surprised that he bought a lemonade for the woman, but he took one, too. And do you know he didn't pay for them? Does that tell you anything about them?'

'Probably forgot,' Dan said.

'I'm going up to my office,' Posey said. 'Come along and I'll show you what we found in the buggy after the accident.'

York took the seat the sheriff indicated when they got to his office.

Posey nodded at two small valises in the corner. 'That's all they had with them. Must not have planned to stay long.'

Dan nodded. Likely they hadn't, if the letter he had was any indication of the welcome they were anticipating. Possibly Renetta intended to take Carlita back with her, so the girl could see Denver.

'What about the circumstances of this wreck?' York asked after he'd looked through the valises without finding anything unusual.

Posey shrugged as Dan sat down again. 'Nothing unusual that we could see. The team just seemed to get too close to the edge and slipped off.'

Dan leaned forward. 'You don't believe that, do you? My pa was a very good driver. And did you ever see a horse that would deliberately go close enough to a drop-off like that to fall over?'

Posey was slow in answering. 'Can't say that I have. Maybe something spooked them.'

York nodded. He watched the face of the stocky sheriff as the lawman's eyes darted around the room.

'I'm sure something spooked them,' Dan said. 'Deliberately spooked them. But you seem to think there's no possibility of murder.'

'I wouldn't say that,' Posey said quickly. 'There have been a couple of murders in the Trap. We caught one of the killers. We figure another fellow, Ike Hamm, who owned the Foolhardy Mine there, was killed, too, but we couldn't find out who did it. Two others died there, but both were drunks and we figured they just wandered too close to the edge and fell over.'

Dan leaned forward in his chair. Posey was talking too much and saying too little. 'I'm not interested in those who died there before. I'm interested in this buggy that went off that road about five weeks ago.'

Posey nodded. 'I know. I wish I could help you, but there is nothing to indicate that it was anything but an accident. Maybe there was a deer on the road that startled the team. After all, the horses were unfamiliar with the road. And it was new to your pa, too.'

York knew the sheriff was making sense, but he had a gut feeling that the lawman was wrong. And he had to keep acting on that gut feeling.

'You wouldn't be backing off for fear it really might be murder, would you?' Dan said.

Posey jerked himself upright in his chair. 'Of course not! If I thought it was murder,

I'd be after the murderer right now.'

Dan stood up. 'So you're going to sit on your fanny till somebody proves it was murder before you do anything. I'm going to assume it was murder until somebody proves it was an accident.' He wheeled out of the office, leaving Posey staring after him with an open mouth.

'There was no motive,' Posey shouted at Dan as he stepped off the porch.

Dan realized that Posey might have a point. Right now, he wasn't sure he could prove someone had a strong enough motive. But he was determined to learn as much as he could.

He headed down the street toward the bank, a block away. He had only one suspect so far. He knew Sam Frake didn't want Carlita to see her mother, Renetta. It was easy to imagine Frake might kill – or arrange a killing – to get his way. But it might not be so easy to prove that.

Entering the bank, Dan looked around. There were three tellers' windows, but two were closed. Dan guessed that what little routine business the bank did these days could all be handled at this window. A man a few years younger than York was behind the window, an eyeshade perched on his forehead. York guessed he was Omar Perkins.

'What can I do for you?' the man asked,

his round, boyish face spreading in a polite smile.

'Just looking for some information,' York said. 'I understand you see Carlita Frake quite often.'

Perkins's face reddened like a summer sunset. 'I can't see how that is any of your business.'

York nodded. 'You're right, but I want to know several things that may not be any of my business. My name is Dan York. My father was killed in that buggy wreck up in the canyon. Did you know the woman in the buggy with him?'

Perkins shook his head. 'I didn't se her when she was alive. I know that she was Carlita's real mother.'

York sized up the young man on the other side of the window. He wasn't very tall and he looked as if he hadn't lost his baby fat although he was in his early twenties. York was surprised that Omar Perkins knew that much about Carlita's past.

'Did you know Carlita's mother was coming?' York asked.

Perkins shook his head. 'Carlita thought she might come sometime but she didn't know when.'

'Did you know whether Sam Frake wanted her to come?'

'Of course he didn't,' Perkins said. 'None of us who knows Carlita wanted her to come.

She might have wanted to take Carlita back to Denver with her.'

Dan nodded, filing another bit of information in his mind. Omar Perkins had a motive for preventing Renetta York from reaching the Box F. But Dan found it difficult to picture him as a murderer.

'Does Sam Frake want Carlita to stay here?'

'I suppose. I never heard him say. He's raised her like his daughter. I see no reason why he wouldn't want her to stay.'

Perkins had been more open than Dan had expected. He thanked Perkins and turned back to the door of the bank. He couldn't help thinking that Omar Perkins obviously wasn't very busy. There hadn't been a customer in the bank while they were talking.

Just outside the bank, Dan stopped short as Winnie Wagasy, the judge's daughter, walked over.

'Thought I saw you go in there,' she said softly. 'Been waiting for you.'

'I'm surprised to see you,' York said.

'Not as surprised as I am to see you,' Winnie said, falling in step with him as he walked toward the sheriff's office, where he had left his horse. 'Pa said you wouldn't get back from the Box F.'

'Was that why he sent me there?' Dan asked.

Winnie shook her head, her red hair flipping around her face. 'He just didn't want to send the sheriff up there with the body, and he certainly didn't intend to go himself. It just seemed reasonable that you should be the one. You killed Flash.'

'Are they really that much afraid of Sam Frake?'

'He's mean and vicious,' Winnie said. 'He thought that Flash could do no wrong, and Pa expected Sam to go for his gun the second he learned that Flash was dead.'

'At least, your pa was right about that,' Dan said.

'Did you kill him?' Winnie asked.

'Didn't have to,' Dan said. 'He was pretty wild but not totally crazy. He wasn't ready to die right then.'

By now they had reached Dan's horse.

A little pout crossed Winnie's face. 'Do you have to go already?'

'I've got things to do,' Dan said. 'But they're not here in Goldtown.'

Dan left Winnie staring petulantly after him as he headed for the general store, where he bought a few things. Then he rode out of town.

At the bottom of the falls, Dan turned off the road and went over to the wreck again. Lifting boards he hadn't touched this morning, he searched for anything that might give him a clue as to what had happened. He found nothing.

Then he looked around him, and something shiny caught his eye. It was a few feet away from the wreck, but things had likely been scattered in all directions when the buggy crashed here.

Moving over, Dan found the shiny object to be a big button made of some dark-colored bone. It had probably come from the clothes of either Tom or Renetta York. He slipped it into his pocket.

Then suddenly he caught sight of a movement above him, at the top of the falls. His head jerked up. A tall man was up there staring down at him. He looked almost as surprised as Dan was.

Dan recognized him instantly. He was the tall, sullen man who had stood beside Sam Frake when he had delivered the body of Jeff Frake to the ranch. Fred Cluff. That was what Vicarona had called him. The sheriff had said he was Jeff's special friend. He'd be after York's hide, and now he certainly had his chance to shoot.

York had left his rifle on his saddle, and the horse was several yards back from the wreck. Whirling, York dashed for his horse. The rifle at the top of the falls roared. The first bullet fell just in front of York.

CHAPTER FIVE

Dan had expected another shot from above by the time he'd taken his rifle from the boot. But there was no second shot.

Whirling, York swung the muzzle of his own rifle toward the top of the falls. There was no one there. He found it hard to believe that Cluff was gone. Maybe he just didn't have any stomach for a give-and-take fight.

After waiting for a few minutest to make sure Cluff wasn't going to reappear, York slid the rifle back in its boot and swung into the saddle. He headed back to the road and up the narrow ledge toward the top of the falls. As he neared the top he pulled the rifle free again. Cluff might be waiting for him.

There was no sign of anybody in the canyon, though. All the same, York kept the rifle across the pommel of his saddle as he rode the rest of the way out of the canyon.

Riding slowly, Dan reached Nugget in the middle of the afternoon. He passed the old livery barn where he had decided he would leave his horse. There was still hay there and it was roomier than the barn where he'd stabled his animal last night.

Today Dan decided to talk to Horace Trill-ingham. The Englishman wasn't as talkative as Vicarona, but he might unknowingly give Dan some important information about the wreck.

As Dan had surmised, Trillingham had chosen the mansion among the houses in Nugget when the residents had moved out. It was a fair distance from Vicarona. A barn behind the house was the only building really close to it. Also close to the mansion was a steep slope.

Trillingham saw Dan coming and came outside the house to meet him. 'Did you have a good day?' he asked.

'Fair,' York said, dismounting. 'Cluff shot at me once from the top of the falls, but that didn't really surprise me. What did surprise me was that he didn't stay and fight. Any idea why?'

Trillingham's brow furrowed. 'Did you shoot back?'

'I had to run to my horse to get my rifle.'

Trillingham nodded. 'By that time, he was gone? That figures. I wouldn't call Fred Cluff a coward. But he's always looking for an advantage. If he doesn't have it, he'll wait until he can get it.'

Dan asked, 'You think he left because he lost his advantage?'

'Precisely,' Trillingham said. 'Shooting straight down isn't easy, you know. You overshoot. But he'll keep trying. Jeff Frake was Cluff's best friend. Cluff is a mean man.'

Dan started toward the door of the mansion, but Trillingham was standing in his way and he didn't move. York stopped.

'You're not going to invite me in?' he asked.

'Some other time,' Trillingham said nervously. 'I like to have my house look decent. Right now a self-respecting pig wouldn't go in.'

'I'm not a pig,' Dan said with a grin, but Trillingham didn't budge.

Dan turned back to his horse. This was something he hadn't expected. Maybe the Englishman just didn't allow anyone inside his house. What could he have in there that he didn't want people to see?

Putting his horse in the old livery barn, Dan walked down to Vicarona's house. Maybe he wouldn't be welcome here, either.

The dark-complexioned man not only threw open his door, but he motioned Dan inside. 'What did you learn today?' he asked eagerly.

Dan told him about examining the buggy, but he said nothing about the letter. 'Cluff took one shot at me from the top of the falls, then lit a shuck,' he said. 'Trillingham thinks he got cold feet when he missed.'

'Likely,' Vicarona said. 'He figures he'll get a better chance.'

Dan took out the dark button he'd found. 'Ever see anything like this? I found it near the buggy. Probably belonged on the clothes of my father or stepmother.'

'Maybe,' Vicarona said, taking the button and looking closely at it. 'Fred Cluff's got a shirt with buttons like that.'

'Maybe Cluff caused that wreck,' Dan said.

'It's possible, but it's more likely he was just poking around the wreck later to see what he could find.'

York filed that bit of information away, too. The list of suspects was growing, but none eclipsed Sam Frake.

'I'm convinced that wreck was murder,' Dan said. 'No team would plunge over a cliff like that without being pushed.'

Vicarona nodded slowly. 'Maybe you're right. Don't seem like a horse that wasn't locoed would go over a cliff. But it still could have been an accident.'

'Assuming it was murder, though, who would be your choice for the one who did it?'

'Don't rightly know since I hadn't thought of it that way. Sam Frake would do it if he thought it was important. Killing a man don't mean no more to him than squashing a bug. I'd say the same is true of Lennie Swift. He's a mean little cuss.'

'Why would he do it?'

Vicarona shifted his feet uncomfortably. 'Maybe I'm throwing suspicion his way when he don't deserve it,' he said. 'But I heard some things. I know for a fact that he's sweet on Carlita. She don't want nothing to do with Lennie, but that don't stop him. Then I heard that the woman in that wreck was Carlita's real mother. I think that maybe she was coming to take Carlita away to the city. Lennie Swift could have done it to stop her from taking Carlita from the canyon.'

Dan nodded. 'That's possible. But how did you hear all this? Who told you?'

'Nobody told me right out,' Vicarona said. 'But Carlita said her mother, meaning Gene- vieve Frake, had hinted that she might get to go to Denver one of these days to live a while. And I heard Sam Frake exploding one day about his worthless sister-in-law. He was speaking about Carlita's real mother, I figured. He said they'd heard she was coming one of these days.'

'And he didn't want her to come, I take it.'

'He sure didn't,' Vicarona said. 'He might have run her off the cliff himself to keep her from getting to the Box F. Or Swift might have taken it on himself to see to it she didn't get here and take Carlita back to Denver with her.'

Dan nodded. If he could prove that Renetta York had been coming to take Carlita away with her, he'd have a motive for Swift committing the crime. Dan wasn't sure that would be a strong enough motive for Sam Frake – though there was the money angle, the marriage to the young banker.

'Does Sam Frake think a lot of Carlita?' York asked.

Vicarona shrugged. 'Not so much, I reckon. All his devotion was wrapped up in that worthless son of his, Jeff. Most people called him Flash. He was a worthless flash in the pan, if you ask me.'

'I'll do some more looking down in the canyon,' Dan said. 'I might find something that will point the finger at the guilty party. And my gut keeps telling me there is a guilty party.'

'You might find something you don't want to find, too,' Vicarona said. 'Old Ike Hamm's mine is down there, not far from the falls. A lot of people are still snooping around trying to find Ike's gold.'

'What exactly happened to Hamm?'

'He was pushed off the cliff there. Some say he just fell, but I reckon he was pushed. He dug a fortune out of his Foolhardy Mine. Nobody can find where he hid his gold.'

'What does that have to do with me poking around that wreck?' Dan asked.

'Nothing, if everybody knows you're looking at the wreck and not hunting for Ike's gold. A lot of people, including me, would love to get their hands on that gold.'

64

'What's to keep somebody from digging more out of his mine?'

'There ain't any more in there. At least, not worth digging out. We figure Ike hit a pocket of almost pure gold. He was barely existing till he hit that gold. Suddenly, he had gold nuggets like you wouldn't believe. Then he just quit mining. I figure he had all he needed and didn't have to work anymore. Somebody figured the same, I reckon, 'cause he was found dead one day at the foot of the falls.'

'I don't see how that's going to affect me in looking for the killer who got that buggy off the road,' Dan said.

'I told you a lot of people are still looking for Ike Hamm's gold. If they think you're doing the same, they might get close – with a rifle bullet.'

'Including you?'

Vicarona shook his head. 'I know what you're doing there, but others might not. Besides, I've looked everywhere down there. I went into his mine. Found a big pocket where it looked like an underground river might have run at one time. I'm guessing Ike found his gold right there. When he had it all dug out, he quit. But I never found anything.'

'Maybe his murderer got the gold,' York suggested.

'I don't think so. Neither does anyone else. Ike was a peculiar old cuss. Wouldn't let anyone come near his mine while he was alive. He wouldn't even let anyone go down in the canyon near his mine. We all figure he stashed his gold somewhere near his mine.'

'Is this mine very close to the wreck?' Dan asked.

'Fairly close,' Vicarona said. 'Ike's cabin isn't far from there, either. I went over it with a fine-toothed comb and didn't find his gold. Maybe somebody beat me to it, but I doubt it.'

Dan went outside to consider what Vicarona had told him. He liked Vicarona and knew that the man was trying to warn him about some new danger he might be in.

His eyes ran over the valley and down the road toward Nugget Canyon. Then he shifted his eyes and caught a glimpse of a rider between town and the Box F. Dan's nerves tensed. If Sam Frake discovered that he was staying right here in his valley, he'd come down on Dan like a bird on a bug.

'Somebody is coming from the Box F,' Dan called back to the house.

Vicarona stepped outside and shaded his eyes as he looked to the northwest. 'That's Carlita,' he said. 'She comes down here almost every evening. Usually brings Horace and me some goodies. Neither one of us is a fancy cook.'

The tension eased in Dan. He couldn't totally relax at the thought of seeing anyone from the Box F, but he was sure he had the least to fear from Carlita Frake.

'If she sees me, will she tell Sam Frake?' York asked.

Vicarona shook his head. 'Not if I tell her Sam doesn't need to know,' he said confidently. 'There ain't a finer person on this earth than Carlita.'

York grinned. Carlita was a saint to both Vicarona and Horace Trillingham. Dan stayed outside the house with Vicarona as the rider came closer. It went against his nature to hide.

Before the rider reached the edge of town, Dan had recognized Carlita. He was surprised at how well he remembered her from the one look he'd had out at the Box F. She cut away from the road and splashed across the creek just below Vicarona's house.

Soon Carlita reined up in front of Vicarona and dismounted, her eyes barely leaving Dan. 'I didn't expect to find you here,' she said.

It was the first time he'd heard her speak, and her soft, musical voice was just what he'd expected. It fit the rest of her. He found himself staring. Her eyes were a velvet black that matched her raven hair, which was now whirled up in a bun that went under her hat. Dan guessed her hair would fall below her waist if she let it down. Her lips turned up at the corners, as if a smile was just a whisper away.

'I have some unfinished business here,' Dan said.

'It will be finished in a hurry if Pa finds you,' Carlita said. 'He's fit to be tied.'

'What about Jeff?' Vicarona asked.

'We buried him last evening at sundown behind the house,' Carlita said. 'Pa has been vowing vengeance, but he thought he'd have to go to Denver to get it.'

Smoothing her divided skirt, Carlita turned to the saddlebags and took out a package rolled in brown paper. She unwrapped it and handed Vicarona a loaf of bread and a huge piece of cake.

Vicarona thanked her, then turned to York. 'See why we call her the angel of Nugget?'

He turned into his house and Carlita started toward the mansion, leading her horse. Dan fell in step with her. Trillingham was already out of his house and coming toward them like a cow heading for the hay wagon. He was equally grateful for his bread and cake and immediately went back inside.

Dan stayed with Carlita as she turned toward the west edge of town. He felt as if he wanted to walk forever beside this girl. Seeing the joy on the faces of the old men of Nugget and knowing how much pleasure she had brought them added to York's appreciation of Carlita.

At the edge of town, Carlita stopped. 'You

mustn't come any farther. If Pa sees you, he'll turn the valley upside down to get to you.'

'Your pa must be a wild man,' York said.

'He's not really my pa,' Carlita said. 'Pa and Mama adopted me.'

'Do you know who your real parents were?'

'My mother was Mama's sister. I didn't get to know my pa. Mama said he left my mother shortly after I was born. Then they were divorced. She was killed in a buggy accident in the Trap just last month.'

Dan nodded. She knew more than he had expected her to. 'My pa was killed in that same wreck. Actually, you are my stepsister.'

She giggled like a child, then smiled softly. 'That's silly, isn't it? I never saw you till yesterday.'

'You're going to see a lot more of me if I have any say about it,' he said.

Her smile faded. 'You must never come near the Box F. Pa really means to kill you. And Fred and Lennie will shoot you if they get the chance.' Her eyes dropped. 'But I come down here to Nugget most days. I – I could come every day while you're here.'

'I'd like that,' Dan said impulsively. 'I'll try to be here.'

Then he remembered what he had come to this country for. He had over two thousand dollars in cash to give to Carlita as well as a deed to a half interest in the foothills ranch. He also remembered that Vicarona and Trillingham had warned him that Sam Frake would take anything away from Carlita that he gave her. Dan certainly had no intention of letting that two thousand fall into Sam's Frake's hands.

'I hear that your pa handles everything at the Box F, including personal things,' York said.

Carlita nodded. 'Mama and I aren't allowed to have anything of our own except clothes. Even then, he tells Mama what to buy.'

Dan decided not to mention the inheritance till he could be sure she would get the good of it. 'Does Frake hurt you?' he asked.

'Mostly ignores me,' Carlita said. 'I'm something he has to put up with.'

'How long before you'll get away from the Box F?' he asked.

'I don't know,' she said. 'Maybe soon.'

'Does Omar Perkins figure in that?'

Her eyes widened. 'You've heard about him?'

Dan nodded. 'Joe Vicarona told me.' Then he added mischievously, 'What's Omar got besides good looks and money?'

She giggled again. 'Not much maybe.' Then her face sobered. 'It is a way to get off the Box F.' She swung onto her horse. 'I'll see you next time I come if you're still here.'

She kicked her horse into a lope across the

valley. Dan wished he hadn't mentioned Omar Perkins. Things had been going so smoothly up till then. York was sure that Carlita liked him. He knew that he liked her. There was no doubt in York's mind, however, that Perkins figured prominently in Carlita's plans.

He turned back into town. He'd talk to Vicarona and Trillingham again. Especially Trillingham – Vicarona had already talked a lot. He might learn something that would pin his father's murder on Sam Frake. That would release Carlita from the threat that apparently hung over her head while she stayed on the Box F. She had never known real freedom of choice in anything, if he was guessing right.

Vicarona met Dan as he came past his house. 'Where are you heading?' he asked.

'Want to ask Trillingham a couple of questions,' York said.

'Come on in my place,' Vicarona said. 'You can talk to Horace later.'

York saw the urgency in his face. 'Have you two had a fight?' he asked.

Vicarona shrugged. 'Of course not. Why?'

'You seem to be trying to keep me from going to his place.'

'Nonsense.' Vicarona took York's arm and propelled him toward the house. 'I just get lonesome. You're good company.'

York frowned. Vicarona obviously didn't

want him to go over to the mansion. He remembered how Trillingham had refused to let him come in earlier. Something was definitely not right and Vicarona had every intention of seeing that Dan didn't find out what it was.

CHAPTER SIX

Dan's questions brought little that was new from Vicarona. The answers did tend to strengthen his conviction that Sam Frake was the man responsible for the deaths of Tom and Renetta York. If not Frake, then one of his hired hands, likely Lennie Swift. Swift had more motive for the crime than Fred Cluff.

They had eaten supper together and talked for hours. It was getting late. Twice Dan got up to leave, but each time Vicarona found some excuse to hold him there. Patience was not one of York's strong virtues.

'Maybe you don't go to bed till midnight,' Dan said finally, getting up from his chair again, 'but I do. I'm going home now and going to bed.'

'Sure,' Vicarona agreed quickly. 'You should be home and sound asleep in five minutes.'

York went out the door, thinking that Vicarona was telling him to go straight home. That was the last thing he intended to do. The longer he stayed at Vicarona's, the more certain he became that something was very wrong here in Nugget.

Trillingham had virtually pushed him away

from his house this afternoon and Vicarona had practically kidnapped him when he found out Dan intended to go up to Trillingham's this evening. Right now he had more questions than ever to ask the Englishman.

Knowing Vicarona would watch him as he left, Dan turned toward the house he had selected as a temporary home. But when he got to the house, he went past it, then turned to his right and crossed the street. Weeds had grown up in the street this summer although York had been told the town had been abandoned only this last spring. Many had left last summer and fall after the mines played out. The livery barn had been closed for a year, but the final exodus had taken place this spring, leaving only Vicarona and Trillingham. Vicarona had given York little satisfaction when he asked why he and Trillingham had stayed. Vicarona had said that they both liked it here and nothing could be gained by moving somewhere else. In spite of their occasional disagreements, he and Trillingham found their companionship all they needed.

Crossing the street, Dan passed an empty store and headed toward the mansion, which was on a small knoll. There were no lights on in the mansion, but that wasn't surprising, considering the hour.

He went to the barn behind the big house and found Trillingham's horse. He thought there might be another horse around. If someone was at Trillingham's house, there would surely be another horse somewhere. It wasn't likely anyone would walk up the canyon to get here, and there was no other means of transportation to bring anyone to Nugget.

He made a circle to the northwest. At each empty house he looked for a barn. He looked in three barns before he found a horse. There was hay in the manger for the horse, and there were few cracks in the siding of the barn. The best place in town to hide a horse, York thought.

Striking a match and shielding it with his hand, he looked over the animal. It was a brown mare that looked more like a kid's pony than a cowhorse. He studied the brand, a VX. He had never seen that brand before.

Carefully Dan checked the houses near the barn. All were empty. Whoever had ridden that horse into Nugget was staying with Trillingham, he was sure.

The question that throbbed through his mind was why Trillingham was keeping his presence a secret. It was no secret to Vicarona. Vicarona had obviously detained York tonight just to keep him away from Trillingham's place.

York knew this was not the time to knock on Trillingham's door, but he had no intention of spending the night wondering who was here without at least making an effort to find out.

The big house loomed before him like a monster as he approached. If he believed in premonitions, he'd swear there was something or somebody in that house that meant bad trouble for him.

For a fleeting second, Dan fought an urge to get away from there. But Dan York didn't run from anything he couldn't see and few things that he could. If nothing else, curiosity would plague him worse later than having to face some unknown danger now.

Stepping out to the door, he rapped on it. There was no sound inside. He drew back his fist and hammered on the door like a blacksmith on an anvil. Inside, Dan heard a thump, as if somebody's feet were hitting the floor.

While he waited for the door to open, he speculated on what he might see when it did. He expected a light to flare up inside, but none did. Then the door opened a foot and Horace Trillingham stood there in a night shirt that came below the knees. In his hand was a revolver.

'Oh, it's you,' he grumbled, glaring at York.

'Do I get to come in?' Dan asked.

Trillingham let the gun sag in his hand, but he shook his head. 'It's the middle of the night. No time for visiting.'

Before York could get a foot in the door,

76

Trillingham shoved the door shut and York was sure he heard a bolt being slid home on the inside.

Dan stood there, pondering the situation. He had seen the preparedness of Trillingham when he opened the door. He was glad that Trillingham had recognized him. But still he didn't get the feeling that the Englishman was surprised to see him. Vaguely Dan wondered if Trillingham had carried the gun in case it was someone he didn't know or if he was prepared to make sure that York didn't get into the house. Trillingham left little doubt that Dan was in no position to force his way inside while he held that gun.

Reluctantly Dan turned away. Now he was certain there was something very strange going on in the mansion. If Trillingham had been distant and suspicious when he'd first met him, York wouldn't have thought so much about his peculiar actions now. But he had been very friendly, very warm.

None of that warmth was in evidence now. It left York's mind whirling as he sought a logical answer to this sudden change. That puzzle went to bed with him and kept him awake. His natural impatience prodded him to find the answer, but he doubted if that was going to be easy.

While he fried some of the bacon for breakfast that he had bought in Goldtown, he kept shooting glances through the dingy window past the store to the mansion. There was no stir there for some time after York had started eating his breakfast, and then it was only Trillingham coming outside and looking around, as if expecting to see an enemy lurking nearby. Quickly he went back inside.

When nothing else stirred at the big house, Dan debated his next move. It was evident that whoever was staying with Trillingham was important to York. If he wasn't, Trillingham and Vicarona wouldn't go to such lengths to keep him from finding out about him. Dan's impulse was to go up there and force his way inside and see who it was. Reason told him he'd likely have to shoot Trillingham to get inside. It wasn't worth that. If it was someone who was trying to kill York, such as one of Frake's hands, he surely would have made his attempt before this.

His next impulse was to find Carlita and give her the money that was coming to her and tell her about her half interest in the foothills ranch. Then he'd be free to leave. But that thought died when he considered the death of his father at the Trap. He could not let that go unavenged if it had been murder.

Considering ways of unraveling that puzzle, he thought of Sheriff Heck Posey. The sheriff didn't seem like a man who would deliberately dodge a question unless he felt it was going to bring trouble on his head. Maybe Dan could persuade him to help, at least tell him everything he knew about the situation. York was sure that Posey hadn't done that yet.

York went outside into the morning sunlight. He decided to ride down to Goldtown and see if he could stir the sheriff into action. He thought he had found out most of Nugget's secrets except for Horace Trillingham's visitor.

He rode through the narrow canyon toward Goldtown, pausing at the Trap to look down at the wreck. Directly above the wreck he dismounted and studied the ground carefully. The dirt on the road was hard, but he could see what appeared to be faint outlines of wheel tracks turning sharply toward the edge of the cliff. Measuring the two tracks with his eye, he decided they were just about the right distance apart to be the wheels of a buggy. Following them to the edge, he looked at the wreck directly below. Those could be the tracks of the buggy as it made its final plunge. No horses or rigs had traveled close enough to the edge to disturb the tracks there. He'd demand that Sheriff Posey come and look for himself. Only terrified horses would have turned that sharply over the cliff.

He mounted and rode on down the canyon. As he came out in view of Goldtown, he saw a rider just at the edge of town. The rider turned toward him immediately and Dan soon recognized Winnie Wagasy. The tiny redheaded girl pulled up beside him.

'Am I glad to see you,' she bubbled. 'I like big men.'

He nodded and grinned. 'You told me that before.'

'Got a good reason this time,' she said. 'We're having a fund-raiser in town for the benefit of Mrs Doyle and her three kids. Her husband, Kurt, was foreman of the Bell ranch, and he was killed guarding the Trap. Everybody thinks some of the Box F men did it, but we can't prove it.'

'What does that have to do with me?' York asked.

'Well, there's an admission charge to the dance. That money will go to Mrs Doyle. Burr Belling will help some since it was his foreman who was killed, but he won't do any more than anyone else.'

'I reckon I can buy a ticket,' York said. 'May not be able to come, though.'

'Of course, you'll come,' Winnie said positively. 'Nobody except his family really misses Kurt Doyle. He was a hothead and argued with the Box F men here in town. He even warned Sam Frake that he'd never get his cattle through the Trap. So he was asking to be killed. Everybody feels sorry for his widow, though.'

'Was Doyle killed before the buggy accident or afterward?'

'Just a couple of days before,' Winnie said. 'Would you like to see the graves of your pa and ma?'

York nodded. 'She was my stepmother. My own mother died in Denver almost eight years ago.'

Winnie led the way out to the cemetery on a ridge between the town and the mountains to the northeast. The graves were new and marked with wooden markers. York glanced at Winnie and thought he saw tears welling into her eyes. She evidently was an emotional girl. She wasn't one to hide her feelings, that was sure.

He turned back to the graves. They were still new enough that weeds hadn't started growing on the dirt. The markers were only wooden slabs. York would see about getting stones to set at the head of each grave. He wished his father's grave was back in Denver beside his mother's. But he'd rest here forever in this mountain cemetery beside his second wife, Renetta.

With a sigh, Dan turned back toward town. Winnie came with him.

'I'm sorry for you,' Winnie said. 'But I thought you'd want to see the graves.'

'I appreciate it,' York said. 'Is the sheriff in town?'

'He usually is,' Winnie said. 'Takes something pretty important to get him to ride out.'

'Maybe I can give him something important to do.'

The road from the cemetery went past the Wagasy home and Winnie stopped there while York went on to the main street and the sheriff's office beside the courthouse. When York stepped inside, he found the sheriff dozing at his desk.

'Want to take a ride, Sheriff?' York asked.

The sheriff jerked awake. 'Not particularly,' he said. 'Where to?'

'Up the canyon to that spot they call the Trap,' York said. 'I want your opinion on whether that wreck was an accident or murder.'

Posey scowled. 'I don't have to ride up there to give you my opinion. I've already told you it was an accident. You can't find out anything about it now. That happened over a month ago.'

Dan nodded. 'I know, but it still doesn't look like an accident to me. I found some buggy tracks, pretty faint, I'll admit. They seem to take a sharp turn to the left and disappear at the edge of the cliff. What caused the horses to make that very sharp turn?'

'How would I know? We looked at the place right after it happened. We got a lot better look than you can get now. We decided it was just a simple accident.'

'I don't think it was,' Dan said grimly. 'I

intend to find out what really happened and who caused it, with or without your help.'

'You've got my permission to hunt all you want to,' Posey said. 'But I can't waste the county's time beating a dead horse. The case is closed as far as the law is concerned.'

York stared at the sheriff. Granted, he was on the lazy side, but there seemed to be something else holding him back.

'Just assuming that it was murder, who would be a logical suspect?'

'Now you're going out on a limb,' Posey grunted. 'There ain't no suspects for a crime that didn't happen. Nobody had ever seen either one of them two in the buggy. So why would anybody want to kill them?'

'That's what I want to find out. Did you know the woman was Genevieve Frake's sister?'

Posey nodded slowly. 'Yeah, I heard that.'

'Somebody might have known her,' York persisted. 'Does that give you any ideas?'

'Of course not. I know Sam Frake wasn't too excited about her coming. But that doesn't mean anything.'

'Why not? Running that buggy off the cliff would be one way to make sure she didn't get there.'

Posey leaned forward, his hands flat on his desk. 'Would you murder your sister-in-law just to keep her from making a visit?'

'I doubt it,' Dan said. 'But I'm not Sam

Frake. Do you think Frake is capable of murder?'

'What kind of a question is that?' Posey growled. 'If you pulled a gun on him, I reckon he could kill you without batting an eye.'

'Then you think Frake could have done it?'

Posey jumped to his feet, his face losing some of its colour. 'I didn't say that. Of course, he didn't.'

York read fear in the sheriff's face. It began to make sense to him. Posey was afraid even to hint that Sam Frake might be guilty.

'What about this Bell foreman, Kurt Doyle?' York asked. 'Think Sam Frake killed him?'

'Not likely,' Posey said.

'Have you checked it out?'

'What is there to check?' Sheriff Posey was belligerent. 'Doyle was dead in the bottom at the canyon. Shot once. A bullet doesn't leave any clues as to who fired it. Doyle had threatened everybody on the Box F. But just because Doyle had threatened them doesn't prove they killed him.'

'Makes them good suspects.'

'Suspecting and proving are two different things.'

'Especially if the one you suspect is Sam Frake?' Dan said.

Posey's cheeks reddened in anger. 'If Sam Frake was guilty of something, I'd take care of him.'

'I'll remember that when I need to have him arrested,' York said. 'I'm going to find out what really happened when Pa and Renetta were killed.'

'Watch your step,' Posey warned. 'Nosing around can be dangerous.'

'Is that why you never get any farther from this office than the saloon?'

York spun on his heel and stamped out of the office. Sheriff Heck Posey was not going to be any help. York was sure that Posey suspected Sam Frake just as he did. But he wasn't going to do or say anything that would bring Frake's wrath down on his head. Dan had the feeling that Posey might be a good man with the badge if he just had the courage to stand his ground.

York mounted his horse and headed back up Nugget Canyon. He had barely ridden clear of the buildings of Goldtown when he heard a horse pounding up behind him. He turned around in the saddle, his hand darting to his gun. Then he saw it was Winnie and he reined up.

'I forgot to sell you a ticket to the benefit dance Saturday night,' Winnie said.

She reined up close to York and held out a ticket with an admission fee penciled on it. Thinking how scatterbrained Winnie was, York dug out a half eagle and handed it over.

'I can't afford to waste money, so I'll have

to come now,' he said, putting the ticket in his wallet.

'I'm planning on that,' Winnie said. 'I'll bet you're going up to the Trap to poke around. You know Sam Frake is out to kill you for shooting Jeff. Why do you hang around?'

'To find the man who caused the wreck that killed Pa. I'm sure that was no accident.'

'Do you think it was Sam Frake?'

'It looks very possible,' York said.

'I'll help you look,' Winnie said. 'Shall we get going?'

If there was danger, York didn't want Winnie exposed to it. But seeing the determination on her face, he said nothing.

When they reached the bottom of the falls, York turned toward the wreck. They came to the splintered buggy and both dismounted.

Suddenly, Winnie clutched York's arm and pointed to the top of the falls. York shot his eyes upward. Just to the right of the falls was a rider. At first York couldn't identify him. Then he saw that it was Fred Cluff.

'Jeff Frake was Fred's best friend,' Winnie said, still holding his arm. 'Fred will kill you if he gets the chance.'

Cluff disappeared from the edge of the cliff, then suddenly burst out on the road leading down to the floor of the canyon. York didn't need to be told he was facing a showdown with Cluff.

CHAPTER SEVEN

Dan watched Cluff come down the road toward him, expecting him to start shooting any second. His own hand was on his gun. But Winnie stood close to York, giving Cluff a small target if he wanted to avoid hitting her.

'You'd better get back,' Dan snapped.

'He won't shoot if he thinks he might hit me,' Winnie said confidently.

'You think he has that much respect for a woman?'

'He has for this one,' Winnie said. 'If he starts shooting while I'm here, I'll help you cut him down.'

York shot a glance at Winnie. There was no fear there. Maybe she knew something about Fred Cluff that York didn't know. Or maybe she was just braver than he had thought she was.

Cluff didn't seem to be paying any attention to the people below him as he drove his horse down the steep road. Once on the canyon floor, however, he wheeled toward York and Winnie.

He didn't have a gun in his hands and his eyes were on Winnie more than York. He pulled his horse to a sliding halt a few yards away from them.

'What are you doing here with him?' Cluff demanded of Winnie.

'I'm here because I want to be,' Winnie said sharply.

Cluff turned his wrath on York. 'Why did you bring her here?'

'Because she wanted to come,' York said. 'What business is that of yours?'

Cluff calmed down a little. 'We've got some business of our own to settle. Jeff Frake was my best friend. An eye for an eye.'

York tried to push Winnie back. 'Fine with me,' he said. 'You'd better be faster than Jeff was.'

Cluff stopped as if he'd been hit with a club. 'I ain't taking a chance of hitting Winnie,' he grunted.

York saw that Cluff had no intention of touching his gun so he relaxed. 'Any way you like it,' he said.

He watched Cluff closely, expecting him to dive off his horse to wade into him with fists. Instead, Cluff dug his spurs into his horse's flanks, driving him forward. York barely had time to dive away from the lunging horse. Even Winnie had to leap to the other side to avoid the startled animal.

'You idiot!' Winnie screamed. 'Be careful who you're running down.'

Cluff wasn't paying any attention to Winnie now. He jerked on the reins so hard his horse reared. With its head yanked back against its shoulder, the horse whirled completely around before his front feet touched the ground. Then Cluff spurred him savagely and he lunged forward directly at York again.

Dan was prepared for the move this time and leaped to one side. As the horse lunged past him, he caught the bridle and pulled down, digging in his heels. The horse's head came down to his forelegs and his momentum threw him into a somersault. Cluff kicked his feet free of the stirrups and catapulted out of the saddle. He landed with a thud but came to his feet almost instantly.

York watched Cluff cautiously as the horse got to his feet and trotted off, snorting his disgust at the entire proceedings. Thinking that Cluff would surely have the fight jolted out of him by that fall, York waited.

Cluff shook himself like a dog coming out of a river, then focused his eyes on Dan.

'That was a dirty trick,' he growled, breathing hard.

'Any worse than trying to run a man down?' York demanded.

Cluff didn't answer, moving closer as though dazed. Then suddenly, when he was within a few feet of York, he lunged at him, all signs of confusion gone.

'Watch out!' Winnie yelled.

Dan wasn't sure who she was yelling at,

but it made little difference now. Vicarona had told him that Cluff prided himself in his fighting ability.

Cluff was shorter than York, so his reach was not as long, but he was solidly built. York didn't take him lightly. Even though Dan was a big man, he was fast on his feet. He was used to brawls. He'd been involved in many of them.

Cluff was a brawler. He proved that in his first charge.

York deftly avoided Cluff's charge, stinging him with a fist as he moved away. He shot a glance at Winnie. He saw none of the horror or disgust that he had expected. She looked like an excited spectator at a gladiator battle. She would root for the winner, he guessed, whichever one that proved to be.

He focused his attention on Cluff. Cluff's blue eyes were boring into York now, trying to size him up for the kill.

York sidestepped two more bull charges by the big cowboy, then decided he could handle him if he met him head-on. The next time Cluff came at him, it was with more reserve. A flicker of surprise flitted across his face when he saw that Dan was not going to dodge him this time.

Cluff was good with his fists. But while he was launching his assault, Dan was delivering a series of hammer blows. Cluff took three or four, then backed up, using arms and hands to shield himself. Surprise was stamped on his face. Obviously, he had never run into an opponent who could hit with such power.

Dan didn't surge ahead to finish him but moved methodically forward, never letting Cluff quite get his balance. He slammed a fist into Cluff's face that brought blood from his nose. Cluff was a good puncher but had few defenses against a man who could pick his spots to hit. Likely Cluff had not had a lot of experience in defending himself. He'd always been the aggressor.

Dan read the man's eyes as he pushed him back. Realization that Cluff was losing showed first, and then a determination shone through.

Now Cluff suddenly lurched forward, disregarding York's pounding blows. He managed to land one blow on the side of York's head that made Dan's head ring, but York didn't retreat.

Cluff, in his eagerness to punish York, left himself open and Dan moved into that opening. He smashed a fist to Cluff's eye and another to his mouth. Cluff suddenly stopped his attack and covered up again. York switched his attack to the cowboy's middle. That brought Cluff's guard down and York took a good shot at his exposed chin.

Cluff reeled backward, completely off balance. But he didn't go down and York moved in, delivering another blow to his face. Cluff went down that time, wallowing around like a wounded pig, trying to get up.

'You'd better stay there,' York warned. 'And don't try for your gun. That was the mistake Jeff Frake made.'

Cluff stopped struggling and glared up at York through one eye. The other was already swelled almost shut. 'I'll get you, wait and see.'

York cocked his fist and, when Cluff cringed away, he stooped quickly and yanked Cluff's gun out of the holster.

'I'll keep this away from you for a while,' Dan said. 'Who put you up to coming after me? Sam Frake?'

Cluff scowled. 'Nobody needs to send me after you. Besides, you were with Winnie. I don't allow that.'

'Seems to me she ought to do her own choosing,' York said.

'She has and it ain't you,' Cluff growled.

Suddenly, he lunged at York from his sitting position, hitting York at the knees. Dan thought he had seen every trick in barroom brawls, but this one caught him by surprise.

He was rocked backward and hit the ground hard. As he reared up, Cluff was scrambling toward him, murder in his one open eye. York propped himself up with his left hand and swung his free fist with all his strength. The fist met Cluff coming in, and the crack was like an ax against a tree trunk. Cluff almost left the ground as he flew backward. He sprawled in the dust and didn't move.

York got to his feet, glaring down at Cluff. Cluff was not one to give up easily. He'd remember that. He heard Winnie's running feet and saw her coming toward him.

'Big man, big fighter,' she breathed in admiration. 'Fred has said that nobody could whip him, not even his friend, Jeff.'

'A lot of people overestimate themselves,' York said.

'Let me doctor your bruises,' Winnie said.

'You'd better doctor Cluff's bruises,' York said. 'He's got more than I have.'

He turned and walked to his horse. He could feel the effects of Cluff's blows. The redheaded puncher had proved a better fighter than York had expected and he certainly was more determined.

Mounting his horse, York reined him around toward the road. He glanced back at Winnie, who was standing where he'd left her, as if she couldn't understand what had happened. Not many people turned her down, York guessed, but he just didn't feel like being with anybody now.

As he rode up the steep slope, he looked down. Cluff was stirring and Winnie was attending to him. A pang ran through Dan. He liked Winnie; she was exciting company. He'd have to wait until he saw her next time to find out how badly she thought she had been snubbed.

Up in the canyon above the falls, Dan put his horse to a gentle lope, feeling his bruises a little more. He knew he had a mortal enemy in Fred Cluff now, but Cluff wouldn't challenge him on even terms again. He'd find some way to get the advantage, likely an ambush.

Dan suddenly remembered something he'd seen during the fight. The buttons on the shirt Cluff was wearing were the same as the button he'd found near the wreck. Vicarona had already said something about that, hadn't he? Could that mean anything? Was Cluff a serious suspect in the murder of Tom and Renetta York? York found it hard to put any suspect above Sam Frake.

Maybe Cluff had acted on Frake's orders. More and more it looked like York would have to clean out the Box F ranch to find the killer.

Riding into Nugget, he was met by Vicarona. The Mexican's black eyes raced over York.

'What did you run into, a grizzly or somebody who thought he could lick you?'

'Didn't see any grizzlies,' York said, swinging out of the saddle.

'Sam Frake or Cluff?' Vicarona pressed.

'Cluff,' York said. 'How come you didn't guess Lennie Swift?'

'He ain't big enough to tackle you. And he ain't dumb enough to think he can, either,' Vicarona said.

'Would he follow Frake's orders to get me?' York asked.

Vicarona nodded. 'Likely. But he won't butt his head into a brick wall. How did you make out with Cluff?'

'It'll be a while before he rides comfortably,' York said. 'We just used fists.'

'Should have used a gun,' Vicarona said. 'It will come to that eventually. You may not get an even break next time.'

That only strengthened York's conclusions. If he didn't find some way to get Carlita out of this valley soon, so he could deliver her inheritance, he might not get it delivered at all.

York spent the afternoon nursing his bruises and searching for a plan to give Carlita her inheritance. He had to be sure that Sam Frake didn't get his hands on that money.

He still hadn't hit upon a workable idea when he glanced out the window in the house he was using and saw the object of his speculation riding toward town from the Box F.

As she came closer to town, York left his

little house and went out to the road leading in from the Box F. He saw that Joe Vicarona was already on the road, but Horace Trillingham was not in sight. He must not have seen her coming.

The corners of Carlita's mouth turned slightly upward when she saw York and Vicarona waiting for her.

'A welcoming committee?' she asked. 'Where's Mr Trillingham?'

'Horace will be along,' Vicarona said.

Carlita swung down and reached into her saddlebag and brought out a brown paper bag. 'Mama baked bread today,' she said. 'She let me bring a loaf down here. You'll have to decide how to divide it. I've got some cookies, too. When Mama heats up the oven to bake, she makes good use of it.'

'No doubt about that,' Vicarona said, eyeing the bread and cookies.

He moved over and took the sack from Carlita and motioned the other two to follow him up to the house. York marveled – and not for the first time – at how quickly Vicarona could move on his peg leg.

Carlita ignored Vicarona's invitation and turned to York. 'Do you know what happened to Fred? He looks like he'd had a battle with a bear. He says his horse fell with him.'

'I reckon that's the truth,' York said.

She shook her head. 'From the looks of

your face, you must have been on that horse with him.'

'Not quite,' Dan said. 'I was down at the foot of the falls in the canyon when he came charging down. We had a tussle.'

'And you won. He looks a lot worse than you. What were you fighting about?'

'Cluff seems determined to get some kind of revenge against me. Says Jeff Frake was his best friend.'

Vicarona had stopped and now he came back, his peg leg stamping the ground excitedly. He looked sharply at York. 'Cluff could ambush you to get even for killing Jeff. It would take something more urgent than that to get him to light into you with his fists.'

'I was examining the buggy that went over the cliff,' York said. 'Winnie Wagasy was with me. Cluff seemed to consider that an infringement on his territory.'

Vicarona nodded. 'So that's it! He's hammered a lot of fellows half to death for looking at her. He's got his rope on her, all right.'

'Not a very tight rope, the way she acts,' Dan said.

Vicarona shook his head. 'Don't figure how you licked him. When he's fighting for something like his girl, nobody has been able to touch him.'

'Maybe that goes two ways,' Carlita said, and Dan jerked around at the sharpness in her voice.

'What was she doing there with you?' Vicarona asked.

'It was her idea,' Dan said, suddenly wanting to explain to Carlita that Winnie hadn't been there at his invitation. 'She simply tagged along when I left Goldtown.'

'I hope you had a nice time,' Carlita said, and there was no mistaking the coolness in her voice. Apparently, she didn't like Winnie Wagasy.

'She said she wanted to help me solve the mystery surrounding that wreck,' Dan said.

'Ain't no mystery about it,' Vicarona said sharply. 'The team simply ran off the cliff.'

'I'm sure she was a big help to you,' Carlita said.

York ignored Vicarona and watched Carlita. Her black eyes were snapping now. He would have had to be deaf to ignore the sarcasm in her voice. She was angry and her anger was directed at him.

CHAPTER EIGHT

Vicarona started for his house again. 'Let's divide this and get Horace's share over to him.' He moved away quickly on his peg leg, carrying the sack Carlita had brought.

'I didn't invite Winnie along,' Dan repeated to Carlita as they followed Vicarona to his house. 'She said she wanted to help and I thought she might know something I didn't.'

'Undoubtedly she does,' Carlita said, and he read a double meaning in her words.

She tossed her head, her black hair flipping across her back as she moved faster to catch up with Vicarona. Dan scowled after her. Why should he care what she thought? It was none of her business if he wanted to cut Cluff out with Winnie, which he didn't. Right now, he only wanted to make Carlita understand that he hadn't taken Winnie up to the falls through choice.

'When I left, she was taking care of Cluff,' Dan said as he caught up with Carlita. Then he pinched his lips together. He wouldn't say any more. He was fawning at her. He never thought he'd do that for anyone.

Vicarona reached his house and went inside, Carlita and Dan following. Vicarona divided the cookies into three piles, then cut the big loaf of bread into three parts. It looked to Dan as if he had cut the loaf in half, then divided the one half into two parts. One of these smaller parts he set aside on his own table and the other he handed to York along with one stack of cookies.

'She brought these things for you and Trillingham,' Dan objected.

'We all share in this town,' Vicarona said. 'Ain't that right, Carlita?'

Her mouth was a thin, straight line across her face as she nodded. York was sure she wasn't happy with Vicarona's decision to share what she had brought with Dan. Well, he wasn't going to humor her anymore. He took what Vicarona had handed him and walked back to his house, putting it on his table.

When Dan stepped outside again, he saw Vicarona and Carlita up by Vicarona's house. They seemed to be arguing. Vicarona held the sack that he apparently was going to take over to Horace Trillingham. Dan thought of the way the Englishman had been secreting himself the last day and his curiosity rose.

Quickly he moved up to Vicarona's house. 'Need some help getting that over to Trillingham?' he asked.

'I don't,' Vicarona snapped. 'I'm perfectly capable of getting this little dab of bread and cookies over to him.'

'I want to see him,' Carlita said. 'I'll just go along with you.'

York's interest was whetted further as he saw that Vicarona was determined to go alone. Something strange was surely happening at the Englishman's mansion. Vicarona knew about it, but he didn't intend to let anyone else find out.

'We'll all go,' Dan suggested and struck out for the big house. Vicarona was quick to follow, his peg leg digging little pits in the soft spots in the ground between the rocks. Carlita came along, her face showing her displeasure at York's presence. Neither of them wanted him along now, York thought, but that didn't stop him. Maybe this time he'd find out why Horace Trillingham had been acting so strangely.

York was surprised at the speed generated by Vicarona as they neared the mansion. With his wooden stump, he beat a tattoo on the porch of the big house as he reached the door first and knocked. Trillingham answered the knock, opening the door little more than a crack.

'Carlita brought us some grub,' Vicarona said, handing the sack to the Englishman. 'I divided it.'

Trillingham looked beyond Vicarona to Carlita and York. 'Thank you, Carlita,' he said. He sniffed the sack. 'Your cooking has the aroma of the gods.'

He backed away from the door and closed it. Vicarona turned around, obviously not offended by Trillingham's rudeness.

Carlita was surprised. 'I wanted to talk to him,' she said.

'He's not feeling too perky,' Vicarona said. 'Next time you come, maybe he'll be ready for a visit.'

Vicarona turned back toward his own house, but Carlita went on up the slope behind the mansion. Dan chose to go with her although he doubted that she appreciated his decision. They climbed in silence until the slope became so steep they were forced to stop to catch their breath.

They turned and looked down over the town and across the creek toward the Box F buildings.

'It's a pretty place for a town and a ranch,' York said.

She nodded absently, as if she were barely aware of his presence. 'I love it here. I can see everything in the valley.'

'Wonder why Trillingham was so anxious to get rid of us,' Dan said.

Carlita brought her eyes away from the valley to look at York. 'I don't know, but I guess it's really none of our business.'

'He seemed plenty glad to get the bread and cookies you brought him. Maybe he has an extra mouth to feed.'

She stared at Dan. 'Who would he have

with him? You have a suspicious mind.'

'That's why I'm still alive,' York said. He thought of saying that she also had a suspicious mind, but he bit back the words.

With a sigh, Carlita started down the slope, and Dan followed. He was certainly off on the wrong foot with Carlita today, but still he had to try to get some answers from her.

'Did your real mother write to you often?' he asked as they passed the mansion.

'No,' she said. 'At least, I didn't get many letters.'

'Do you think Sam might have kept the letters from you?'

She shot a look at him. 'I imagine he did,' she said with a noticeable rancor.

'Do you think your mother intended to take you home with her when she returned from this trip?'

'It could have been the reason she was coming,' Carlita said slowly, as if she wanted to be sure not to say too much.

He wondered how much more she could tell him.

York looked at the windows of the mansion, but the shades were drawn. That didn't make sense in a ghost town like this. His curiosity rose another notch.

'What makes you think that's why your mother was coming here?'

'Mama hinted that my mother was coming.

She said that she lived in Denver and it would be a good place for me to go to see what the rest of the world looked like.'

'Would you have gone?' Dan asked.

As they walked down the dirt street past the smaller houses toward the creek, she shook her head without looking at him. 'I don't know. I wouldn't want to leave Mama. Besides, I love this valley.'

'You'll have to leave here someday,' York said. 'There's nothing here now but this ghost town and the Box F. You're practically cut off from the world.'

'That's not so bad,' she said. 'This whole valley is mine to ride over. If I was in a city, there'd be people real close, Mama says. Like they are down in Goldtown.'

Thinking of Denver, Dan realized what a shock that city would be to this girl who probably hadn't been much farther from this valley than Goldtown. It was too bad that Renetta hadn't had the opportunity to introduce her daughter to the world beyond this place. Carlita had been cheated out of an experience and education that were rightfully hers.

'Mama was doing a lot of sewing for me before that accident,' Carlita volunteered. 'She was getting me ready to go to Denver, I think.'

'What did Sam think of that?' Dan asked.

'He didn't like it. He hated my mother.'

'Did he hate her enough to kill her?' York asked bluntly.

Carlita's mouth dropped open and she stared at him. 'Pa wouldn't do anything like that. You heard Joe Vicarona say it was just an accident.'

York could see how agitated Carlita was, so he changed the subject. He was sure she had told him about all she could, anyway.

'I heard down in Goldtown about the fund-raising dance they're holding for the widow Doyle. Are you going?'

'I might. Omar Perkins has asked me, but Pa hasn't said yet whether I can go.'

'Vicarona said Sam approves of Perkins.'

'He does,' Carlita said. 'But he's not sure about a Frake being at that benefit dance.'

York understood that reasoning. He was surprised at how easily Carlita talked about Omar Perkins. He had expected her to be bashful. Instead, she talked about going to the dance with him the same as she would about going to town with her father.

They wandered along the bank of the creek and up to Vicarona's house where Carlita had left her horse. She swung into the saddle and waved at Vicarona, who thumped out to his porch to see her off.

'Just how serious is this thing between Carlita and Omar Perkins?' York asked Vicarona when Carlita was gone.

'Plenty,' Vicarona said. 'Sam encourages it.

That looks suspicious to me. I don't trust Sam Frake any farther than I can throw a rock. So I went down to Goldtown to check up on Perkins. He's a little fellow, you know, no bigger than me. He's the son of the banker there in Goldtown and he's the next one to take over. His pa ain't in very good health, so he could own that bank just any day.'

'Think that has anything to do with Frake encouraging Carlita to go with Perkins?'

'I figure it has everything to do with it. That bank holds a mortgage on Burr Belling's ranch. Burr is trying to squeeze Frake into a tight spot where he can't wiggle out, then buy out the Box F and this whole valley for a song and sing it himself.'

York was one jump ahead of Vicarona. 'You think Frake plans to get his fingers into some of the dealings of that bank when his son-in-law becomes the owner?'

'Took me a while to put the pieces together,' Vicarona said, 'but that's exactly how I figure it. He'll try to get the bank to foreclose on Belling.'

'If Carlita went to Denver with her mother, she wouldn't marry Perkins,' York said. 'Reason enough for Frake to see to it that her mother didn't get to the Box F.'

Vicarona studied York's face. 'I still say it was an accident,' he said slowly, 'but if it wasn't, that might be just what happened.'

'In Goldtown, they told me that somebody from the Box F killed Kurt Doyle, Belling's foreman.'

'I see nothing wrong with that reasoning,' Vicarona said. 'Belling is determined to see that Sam doesn't get any cattle out of this valley, and Sam is just as determined to get them out. Doyle was in the way.'

'How about Fred Cluff's interest in Winnie Wagasy?'

'Reckon that's real enough,' Vicarona said. 'Winnie's a flirt. Anything wearing pants looks good to her.' His black eyes began to sparkle. 'I saw how upset you were when Carlita turned a cold shoulder after you said you'd been with Winnie. Now if you're thinking about Carlita yourself, you've got plenty of competition. Not only Perkins down in Goldtown but Lennie Swift thinks he has the inside track with her. He's right there on the ranch and he sure is sweet on her.'

'I haven't heard much good about Swift,' Dan said.

'Your hearing's good. I'd a heap sight rather see Carlita get Perkins than Lennie Swift. He's jealous and mean. You have to watch your back when you're around him.'

'I watch everybody from the Box F,' Dan said. 'Does Mrs Frake ever leave the ranch for any reason?'

'She takes a buggy ride every nice day. Won't be long now till winter sets in and she can't get out. Sometimes she drives down here.'

York made a mental note of that. He thought of the oncoming winter. Frake would have to get rid of some of his cattle before then.

'What will Frake do about selling his cattle this year?'

'I don't know. I don't think Sam knows, either. He used to sell right here in Nugget, but the market is down in Goldtown now. Belling ain't about to let Sam bring his cattle down there.'

'Frake doesn't strike me as a man who'd knuckle under to anybody.'

Vicarona nodded. 'You can figure on some fireworks before the snow flies.'

York glanced at the sun dropping lower in the west. It would soon disappear behind the mountains on the other side of the valley. He looked up toward the Box F. Carlita's horse was little more than a bump on the road to the ranch. Vicarona had turned and was clumping back into his house. Dan turned up toward the mansion.

Judging from what Trillingham had done this afternoon, he guessed that he wouldn't let him in now, but Dan was going to face him and find out what he could. Reaching the mansion, he stepped up on the porch and crossed to the door.

There was a flurry of activity inside when

York knocked, but he couldn't see through the drawn window curtains to find out what was going on. Maybe the door was unlocked. He was tempted to push it open and look, but that was no way to treat a friend. Up till yesterday, at least, he had considered Horace Trillingham a friend.

Then the door opened just a crack and Trillingham stared out. 'What do you want now?' he demanded.

York looked past Trillingham. He saw a chair halfway across the room with a woman's coat draped over it.

'I want to know who the woman is you're hiding,' Dan said.

Trillingham's eyes widened. 'I say now! You're getting mighty nosy. What makes you think there is a woman here?'

'Since when have you started wearing a woman's coat?'

Trillingham twisted around to look and, as he did, he pulled the door farther open. York stepped inside, crowding past the Englishman.

'Aren't you a little old for secret affairs like this?' York added.

'It's no such thing,' Trillingham snorted angrily. 'She wouldn't be here if Joe wasn't so stubborn.'

'Is she Vicarona's lady friend?' York asked, recalling how nervous Vicarona had appeared when they'd been over here.

'She's nobody's lady friend,' Trillingham snapped. 'She's here on business.'

'Business?' York grunted. 'What business? Does she want to buy a house?'

Trillingham hesitated. 'What's wrong with that? This is a pretty place to live. Joe's just too stubborn to agree to terms.'

'If he's holding out for a high price for a house in Nugget, he's crazier than a bedbug in a blizzard. The lady must be crazy, too. Let me meet her.'

'You tend to your own business. Joe and I will take care of ours.'

York could see the anger rising in Trillingham again. 'Maybe I could help sell her on a house,' he said.

Trillingham's eyes jerked up to the three rifles and a shotgun above the door. 'A man can get killed in this town if he gets too nosy.'

York sized up the Englishman. He was too frail to be much of a factor in a fight, but there was plenty of determination in his face. York doubted if identifying the woman was important enough to risk hurting Trillingham.

'Tell your lady friend I wish her well,' Dan said and backed out the door.

There was no question now in his mind that whoever the woman was, she had some dealings with both Trillingham and Vicarona. Apparently, it was Vicarona's stubbornness that was forcing the lady to stay in Nugget. York would love to know what kind of a deal they were trying to make.

He headed down the street toward his house. It was almost dark now, but he thought nothing of that until he reached the house. Just as he stepped up on his porch, he caught a movement to his left. Wheeling that way, he saw a rider kick his horse into a gallop to the creek and splash across. He was out of sight and range almost before Dan could collect his wits.

York was tired and went to bed thinking that tomorrow he'd better move to another house.

Sometime in the night, Dan was roused out of a deep sleep by the strong smell of smoke. Rearing up in his blankets, he saw the flames licking up one inner wall of the house. Also, there was smoke curling in under the door. The house was burning and the fire was on all sides of him.

CHAPTER NINE

Dan's first thought was that he'd be burned alive. Then the panic vanished as quickly as it had struck him. There was fire at both side windows and smoke at the door. His enemy fully expected to keep him locked in here to burn. But maybe he could still leap through the fire – if he moved before it got any hotter.

He jerked on his clothes and quickly buckled on the money belt with Carlita's money. Grabbing his gun and rolling up his bedroll, he tucked it under his arm except for one blanket, which he threw over his head.

He slammed the door open, and a hot blast hit him. Branches had been piled in front of the door and set on fire. Some were still green, and they were smoldering instead of blazing. That was lucky for him.

Dan leaped across the branches, hitting the ground and rolling over. Whoever had gone to such trouble to burn him in the house would stick around to see that he didn't escape.

A rifle bullet squired dirt in York's face as he rolled. Yanking the blanket off his head, he tried to get his gun out of his holster, but he had stopped rolling with the gun under him.

A bullet nicked York's arm before digging into the dirt just beyond him. Dan rolled over again. The roar of a big gun echoed against the mountain. That meant there were two rifles out here. York realized that his chances were even less than he had calculated.

Both rifles roared again, but no bullets came close to York. Getting his gun free, he rolled to his knees and looked for a target. Flames were leaping higher by the minute from the house, throwing a weird, flickering light over the area.

In one quick sweep, York discovered that the big gun was bellowing from a house half a block away. Vicarona's house. That explained why no bullets had come his way in that last exchange. Down toward the creek, York saw a man on a horse. That must be the man who had set fire to his house and had been firing at him.

Leveling his revolver, Dan fired at the man, but, considering the uncertain light and the distance, he knew it would be a miracle if he hit him. His gun added to the thunder of Vicarona's big rifle, however, was more than the firebug had bargained for and he spurred his horse into the creek, then thundered away.

York put his gun away and turned to the

114

fire. There was nothing he could do to save the house. He thought he had brought out all his things so he'd suffer no personal loss except some scorched skin on his hands.

Vicarona came from his house, wearing a long nightgown that would have made York laugh under different circumstances. He was carrying a big Sharps .50 and that added to the ridiculous sight. But it wasn't ridiculous to Dan. Without Vicarona's intervention, he might be dead now.

'Never heard a prettier sound than that old buffalo gun,' Dan said.

Vicarona grinned. 'I hadn't fired Old Betsy for two or three years. It makes a lot of noise, but I'm not sure I can still hit anything with it.'

'Just hitting the breeze around that fellow's head was all it took to get rid of him. Did you see who it was?'

'There were two of them when I first looked out,' Vicarona said. 'The light from the fire flickering in my window woke me up. Unless I'm getting blind in my old age, it was Sam's two hired hands, Fred Cluff and Lennie Swift. Lennie lit out like a scalded ghost with the first shot I made. Cluff stayed around till you got into the fight. Then he lit a shuck, too.'

'I'd be ready for a hole in the ground if you hadn't taken a hand,' Dan said. 'I won't forget it. What will Sam Frake say about you shooting at his boys? He probably ordered them to burn me out.'

Vicarona nodded. 'Likely. But I'll just remind Sam that he told me and Horace to take care of this town for him. Letting it burn down is no way to take care of it. He'll never admit his boys did it. It's almost morning now. Too late to sleep any more. I'm up for the day, so you might as well have breakfast with me.'

Dan looked at the blazing house. There was no wind and there were no other buildings too close to it. The fire wasn't likely to spread. He did get a bucket and carry water from the creek to soak the grass around the place so the fire wouldn't creep through the grass to some other building.

By the time that was done, Vicarona had breakfast ready and Dan went to his house to eat.

'If you're going to stay,' Vicarona said while they ate, 'the old Jones place at the upper end of town is one of the best houses here.'

'I'll check on it,' York said. 'It looks like I'd better get out of town, though, or you'll get in trouble for letting me stay here.'

Vicarona shrugged. 'I'm not inviting you to stay. You're doing that on your own. For your own sake, though, I'd have to say it would be smart to get out while you're still able.'

'I've got to give that money to Carlita

first,' Dan said.

'Not unless you want Sam Frake to get it.'

York didn't argue the point, but he had been thinking that if he told Carlita to hide the money, surely she wouldn't let Sam Frake know she had it.

Dan walked up to the house in the upper part of town close to the creek. It still had some paint on it and was in better shape than most of the buildings in town. There was some old furniture in this house, too. York put his bedroll inside. It didn't take him long to move in.

As he headed back toward Vicarona's, he saw a buggy coming toward town from the direction of the Box F. Sam Frake wouldn't drive a buggy. He doubted if Carlita would, either. This must be Genevieve Frake. He had been wanting to talk to her. He wouldn't let this opportunity get away.

He angled down below the pile of still-smoking ashes that had been his house. The ford across the creek was only about fifty yards from that. Dan was waiting on the town side of the ford when Genevieve Frake drove her buggy through the creek.

'You still here?' she asked in surprise. 'Sam said you'd be gone.'

'Haven't left yet,' York said. 'Did you come to see the fire?'

She wrapped the lines around the whip stock. 'I came to see which house had burned. I was afraid it might be the mansion. I think that is a beautiful house. I even suggested to Sam that we move into it ourselves, but he won't budge.'

'The house that burned was the one I was trying to live in,' Dan said.

She looked sharply at him. 'Carlita has been seeing you here in town, hasn't she?'

Dan sidestepped her question. 'I have some things to ask you,' he said, wondering just how much he would have to divulge before she'd tell him what he wanted to know. 'Was Renetta York coming here to take Carlita to Denver?'

'She was coming to see Carlita,' she said. 'If Carlita liked her, as I thought she would, then I'd have sent her back to Denver to learn what the real world is like. This valley is beautiful, but it's like living in a feudal system with Sam as the lord of the valley. It's no place for a girl like Carlita.'

Dan nodded. 'I agree with that. Vicarona tells me that she had plenty of friends, especially a young banker in Goldtown. He says that Lennie Swift is fond of her, too.'

Genevieve frowned. 'Lennie is Sam's sister's boy. He's a cousin of Jeff's and, in a way, a cousin of Carlita, but he's no blood relation. I don't like Lennie, and Carlita doesn't, either.' She frowned at him. 'Why am I telling you this? It's none of your business.'

'I'd say it is some of my business. Carlita is my stepsister. I didn't really know her mother but Pa thought Renetta was wonderful. Since she was your sister, I can see why.'

He saw Genevieve's eyes widen, and then a flush crept up her cheeks. Dan guessed it was the first compliment she had received in a long time. It seemed to release a flow of words.

'Renetta made a bad first marriage. We never saw her husband and she didn't tell us much about him. He left her with a tiny baby. There was a divorce. She had to work at any job she could get, and she couldn't take care of the baby, so she asked me to. The only way Sam would let me take the baby was for us to adopt her. Then Sam wouldn't let Renetta even come to see her.'

'That doesn't seem right,' Dan said.

'Nobody said it was,' Genevieve retorted. 'Sam is not one to forgive. Renetta once went with Sam's brother in Texas, you see, and we thought they would get married. But Renetta threw him over and ran off with this other man. Sam's brother took it hard and got roaring drunk. On the way home that night, he fell of his horse. His foot caught in the stirrup, and he was dragged to death. Sam blamed Renetta for his brother's death.'

Dan suddenly had a fuller understanding of Sam Frake's hate for his sister-in-law, but he couldn't see that it was grounds for murder – and he was convinced that was what had happened at the Trap. Then a new thought struck him.

'She evidently was not a poor woman when Pa married her. She had a little ranch in the foothills not too far from Denver.'

'She married again,' Genevieve said. 'She and her second husband had a small ranch. Then he was killed in a stampede. She stayed on the ranch and ran it with two hired hands. I think she was still there when she married your pa. I thought it was time for Renetta to take her daughter out to civilization and let Carlita learn how the world lives.' She wiped a hand across her face. 'I'm to blame for Renetta's coming here and – and getting killed.'

'Don't blame yourself,' Dan said. 'If it was an accident, it wasn't your fault. If it was murder, somebody else was to blame for that. Pa and Renetta made out a will. I came here to give Carlita her share, which is considerable.'

Genevieve's mouth formed a round O. 'So that's what you're doing here! I was sure that you hadn't just wandered into Goldtown. I don't know about giving Carlita any money. Sam runs the finances at the ranch.'

'Vicarona told me that Sam would take any money I gave Carlita. That sounds ridiculous.'

'It isn't,' Genevieve said. 'He handles every-thing. But that situation will change for Carlita one of these days.'

'When she marries the banker in Gold-town?'

'If not before,' Genevieve said. 'I'm not sure about Omar Perkins, either.' She clucked to the team. 'I'm going to take a closer look at that burned house.'

Dan let her drive on. He wanted to check at the bank in Goldtown. Sam Frake's motive for stopping Carlita's mother from getting to Nugget might very well have been to keep Carlita in the valley so she would marry Omar Perkins. Then through his son-in-law, he'd get his hands in that bank and destroy Burr Belling. That, combined with his want-ing to avenge his brother's death, made plenty of sense.

Dan suddenly thought of the fund-raiser in Goldtown. That was tonight. He'd go early and see what he could find out before the dance.

Genevieve had not left Nugget yet when Dan saddled his horse and rode toward the canyon. At the Trap, he stopped, staring down at the buggy from the ledge. He couldn't make himself believe that had been an accident. He rode down to the wrecked buggy near the waterfall and got down to examine it again.

Suddenly, dirt spurted into the air a

couple of feet from him. The next instant, the explosion of a rifle reverberated back and forth between the walls of the canyon. Jerking his head up toward the top of the falls, Dan saw a small man with a rifle at his shoulder. Lennie Swift!

Another shot spanged into the dust just beyond York. Shooting almost straight down. Swift was overshooting his target. But he'd correct his error soon. Dan knew he couldn't ride out without getting hit. His best bet was to get up against the cliff where Swift would have an even more difficult angle. York's rifle was in the boot on his saddle. He'd learn to carry that rifle in his hand when he came here.

Dodging back and forth, he charged toward the falls. Reaching the wall, he saw that there was quite a space between it and the water where the falls hit the floor of the canyon. Without hesitation, York dodged in between the water and the wall. Lennie Swift would have no target now.

Suddenly, his mind was jerked away from Lennie Swift. In the dim light under the falls, Dan saw a hole running into the cliff. It was odd that there would be a hole here where water didn't hit, only the mist. Running his hand into the dim interior of the hole, which was about a foot and a half square, he felt his fingers touch some sacks. He could feel four or five separate sacks. He gripped one and brought it out into the weak light. It was a canvas bag covered with mildew. Before long, the dampness would rot the canvas.

Untying the thong that held the mouth of the sack closed, he looked inside. Immediately he knew what he'd found. The gold dust and tiny nuggets gleamed dully. This had to be the gold Ike Hamm had taken from his Foolhardy Mine. According to what Dan had heard, nobody had found his gold after he had been pushed off the cliff.

Giving it a quick thought, York tied up the canvas sack and pushed it back into the hole where he'd found it. Right now, his concern lay with getting Carlita's inheritance to her and in solving the puzzle surrounding his father's death. Once those two jobs were out of the way, he could come back and get the gold. It had been safe here for a long time; it would be safe a while longer.

Dashing out from under the falls, he lifted his gun and stared at the top of the falls. Lennie Swift was there, peeking over. The range and angle were bad, but York fired twice and Swift disappeared like magic. Running to his horse, Dan wheeled to look up. Swift was not in sight. Mounting, York rode his horse to the road and headed up to the Trap.

At the top of the falls, he looked for the Box F hand. Swift had disappeared. Apparently, he had no stomach for facing a man who would shoot back at him. York stared up the canyon for a moment, then turned his horse and went slowly back down the steep road toward Goldtown.

Once there, he rode directly to the bank. The more he thought about the possibility that Frake could somehow gain control of the bank through Carlita's marriage to Omar Perkins, the more it sounded reasonable that this was Sam Frake's motive for murdering Tom and Renetta York.

The small black-eyed Omar Perkins was at the window when York stepped inside. York wasted no time in preliminaries.'

'Has Sam Frake ever asked you about the business of the bank?' he asked.

Perkins stared at York as if he'd lost his mind. Then his eyes squinted. 'What business is that of yours?'

'I'm not sure yet. I'm trying to piece some things together. You haven't answered my question.'

Perkins frowned. 'I'm not sure that I should. He hasn't gotten personal, but he has asked about the well-being of the bank. What's wrong with that?'

'That depends on why Frake wanted to know how the bank was doing. Maybe he has ideas of you loaning him money if he can't get his cattle down here to sell them.'

Perkins shrugged. 'That's a possibility, I guess.'

York wheeled out of the bank, leaving a puzzled young banker behind. York felt he was a step closer to convicting Frake.

He swung into the saddle and rode to the sheriff's office. Posey might shed some light on things. The sheriff was on the porch of his office, watching York approach.

'I suppose you have more questions about that wreck?' Posey asked cautiously.

York shook his head. 'Wanted to ask your opinion on the possibility of a range fight between Frake and Belling.'

'It's going to happen and it will be a real war,' Posey said.

'Would it be if Sam Frake controlled the bank here in Goldtown?'

'Fat chance of that!' Posey said. 'He couldn't buy an old setting hen. Belling has him trapped up in that valley. He'll never get his cattle past the Trap.'

'You figure Belling will win the war when it starts?' Dan asked.

'No other way. Belling has more men and more guns, and Frake will have to bring his cattle down past the Trap.'

'Just supposing Sam Frake did control the bank here. What would that do to Belling?'

'Ruin him,' Posey said without hesitation. 'Belling owes his shirt to that bank. Don't reckon Burr has anything to worry about though.'

'Probably not,' York said and headed for

125

the saloon.

York got into a card game at the Lucky Strike and it was sundown before he realised it. He went outside, thinking about supper before the dance started. He turned toward the hotel next door but stopped when Winnie Wagasy called to him from across the street.

'No supper at the hotel tonight,' she said, as if reading his mind. 'The dining room has been cleared for the dance tonight. Come on up to our place. I'll find something for you. After all, I don't want a hungry man to take me to the dance.'

'I supposed you'd be going with Cluff. Or maybe he won't come down.'

'He'll be there,' Winnie said as she started toward the Wagasy home behind the bank. 'I can go with him any time. I want to make sure you have a good time. First time you've been to one of our dances.'

York followed her more because she seemed to leave him no option than because he wanted to eat at the judge's house.

At the house, he found the judge gone, stuck in a town in another valley with a trial that hadn't yet ended.

'He wanted to be here for this fund-raiser,' Gilda Wagasy said, 'but duty comes first.'

Gilda Wagasy set out a tasty meal. It was dark when York finished eating. Winnie was impatient to get to the hotel.

'Will Omar Perkins bring Carlita tonight?'

126

York asked, wondering if Sam Frake would let her come to this affair, even with Perkins.

'Fred Cluff will bring her down,' Winnie said. 'Omar can't get off work in time to go after her. But he'll take her home. Fred brings her down, then Omar takes Carlita, and Fred takes me. A good setup.'

York had thought he might enjoy the evening, but if Fred Cluff was going to be there, he doubted he would. Dan didn't want Carlita to see him with Winnie Wagasy, either. She hadn't gotten over the fact that Winnie had been with him when he had fought Cluff. How would she react if she saw him with Winnie tonight?

And how would Belling's hands react when they saw Cluff? It would be a miracle if the evening didn't erupt into a war.

CHAPTER TEN

In the lobby of the hotel, Dan stopped. 'Shouldn't you wait for Cluff?' he asked Winnie.

She shrugged. 'Why? I'll see him later. Right now I want to make sure you have a good time.'

'Last time I met Fred Cluff, we had a difference of opinion.'

'I remember.' Winnie smiled. 'Maybe you will again. It would liven things up.' A shadow passed the window and Winnie pointed. 'Here comes Omar.'

The young banker came into the lobby and Winnie began talking to him. Dan slipped outside, moving into the shadows at the side of the hotel. If Cluff did bring Carlita, as Winnie said he would, then he'd just ride back to Nugget. If he went back inside, Winnie might put on a show of looking after the newcomer. Dan knew how that would affect Carlita.

Of course, it made no sense for him to worry about what Carlita thought. She was going to be with the banker's son, Omar Perkins, tonight and they were to be married before long.

Within five minutes, Dan saw a buggy come down the main street and pull up in front of the saloon next door to the hotel. Every space in front of the hotel was already taken. A man got out and tied the team. The light was poor, but York recognized Fred Cluff.

Cluff helped Carlita out of the buggy, and they came over to the hotel. After they turned into the lobby, York moved around the corner where he could see inside. Just as Winnie had predicted, Carlita paired off with Omar Perkins and Cluff went over to claim Winnie. York was glad that he had decided to step out of the picture.

Dan started toward his horse hitched in front of the saloon but stopped when Gilda Wagasy called to him from across the street.

'Just a minute, Mr York.' She hurried over to him. 'I've heard you're interested in that buggy wreck up at the Trap. There is a man who will likely be here tonight who saw that wreck.'

'The wreck that killed my pa?' York asked in astonishment.

Gilda nodded. 'He's one of Burr Belling's hands. He was up there on guard that day to make sure that Sam Frake didn't try to bring his cattle down to Goldtown.'

'What did he see?' Dan asked.

'I have no idea. I just know that he saw the wreck. In fact, I don't think he's told

130

anybody what he saw. Maybe he's afraid to tell. But I thought you ought to know. Maybe you can get him to talk.'

'What's his name?'

'Peter Aurbitter. Stick with me, and if I see him, I'll point him out.'

York's determination to ride out of town vanished. If somebody had seen that wreck, he'd know exactly what had happened. From what Gilda had said about the man not talking, Dan was convinced that it must have been murder. Probably the man could identify the one who had caused the wreck.

Without hesitation, he walked into the big room with Gilda, his eyes running over the crowd. Other than Fred Cluff and Omar Perkins, he didn't see a man that he knew. And the only women he recognized were Winnie and Carlita.

'See him anywhere?' Dan asked Gilda softly.

She glanced up at him and smiled. 'He's here. I was sure he would be. He's that slim man over near the door to the kitchen.'

York looked. The man would be easy to lose in a crowd. He was of medium height, with brown eyes and brown hair. York couldn't see anything distinctive about him, but he studied his face so he'd recognize him when he got the opportunity to talk to him.

The musicians were just tuning up their

fiddles. The dance would soon begin. York debated whether to bull his way across the floor to Aurbitter now or wait until he might be less conspicuous.

'Is this Aurbitter anything special on the Bell ranch, like a foreman?' Dan asked.

'Kurt Doyle was the foreman,' Gilda said. 'Pete is just one of the riders. But he was the one who saw the wreck.'

Dan impulsively decided there would be no better time to approach the Bell hand. He started into the crowd, then saw that Aurbitter was coming his way, so he waited.

As he passed, Dan reached out and touched his sleeve. 'Mr Aurbitter, could I talk to you for a minute?'

'You sure picked a bad time, cowboy,' Aurbitter said, turning to stare at York. 'I was just after a partner for the first dance.'

'They'll be dancing all evening,' York said. 'I need to talk to you.'

For a moment, Dan thought he was going to have to back off or face a fight.

Aurbitter evidently had his eye on a girl and didn't want to be sidetracked. 'All right,' he said finally, 'but make it fast.'

York stepped to the edge of the crowd and Pete Aurbitter followed him. 'I understand you saw a wreck at the Trap about a month ago,' Dan said.

Aurbitter glared at him. 'So what if I did?'

'I want to know what you saw,' Dan said.

'Just who are you, mister?' Aurbitter demanded.

'I'm the man who shot Jeff Frake,' York said. He expected that to make a strong impression on the Bell cowboy and he saw immediately that it did.

'Name's York, ain't it?' Aurbitter said. 'Just what do you want to know?'

'Who forced that buggy off the cliff?' York said.

'Well, I'll tell you,' Aurbitter began. 'I was guarding against Sam Frake bringing his beef down to Goldtown. It was a pretty dull job. Then I heard this buggy coming from Goldtown. I got out of sight because I didn't know who it might be. If it was somebody from the Box F, he might plug me if he saw me. And there wasn't liable to be anybody else going on to Nugget. That's a ghost town now, you know.'

'I know,' York said impatiently. 'I want to know what you saw.'

Just then Winnie came bouncing over as the music started. She grabbed York's arm.

'Come on,' she said. 'We need one more couple to make a square. Molly doesn't have a partner. Come on.'

York was dragged away from Aurbitter, who seemed as eager to get away as Winnie was to get another couple for her square. York was seething. He had almost heard the report of an eye witness to the buggy wreck.

133

He could have cracked Winnie's neck for butting in.

Molly proved to be a better dancer than York, but he wasn't thinking about the dance and barely heard what the caller was shouting above the scrape of the fiddles and the shuffling of dozens of feet.

As soon as the dance was over, York moved back to the wall where he could survey the floor. Before he located Aurbitter, another set had started, and York had to wait until it ended. He got his eye on Aurbitter, who apparently had come here for only one thing: having a good time.

As soon as the music stopped, York cut through the crowd to Aurbitter. Catching his arm, he pulled him toward the edge of the throng.

'We didn't finish our talk,' he said.

'I ain't finished dancing, either,' Aurbitter said angrily. 'I came here to dance.'

'As soon as you tell me what you saw, I won't bother you anymore,' York said.

'I ain't told anybody what I saw,' Aurbitter said.

'You started to tell me. It was my pa who was killed in that wreck. I think I have a right to know who did it.'

Aurbitter's long face sobered. 'I reckon you do,' he said. 'I'll be glad to tell somebody. It's been mighty hard to keep it bottled up inside.'

'Well,' York prodded. 'What did you see?'

York heard Winnie's call from ten feet away. He swore under his breath. She was going to break in again. Pete Aurbitter wasn't going to say anything while anyone was within hearing distance.

'We're short a couple in a square again, Dan. Come on.'

Directly behind Winnie came Fred Cluff like a calf following its mother. The sight of Cluff was a red flag to Pete Aurbitter.

'It must take a lot of nerve for a Box F puncher to come to a fund-raiser for the widow of the man they killed,' Aurbitter snarled, glaring at Cluff.

Cluff bristled like a cornered dog. 'Watch your tongue, buster! I didn't kill anybody.'

'I ain't taking it back,' Aurbitter said. 'The Box F killed Kurt Doyle.'

Cluff lunged at Aurbitter. There wasn't room in the crowd for flying fists. It developed into a wrestling match almost instantly. York watched for a moment. If something happened to Aurbitter, he wouldn't find out who had caused that wreck at the Trap, and Cluff was a much bigger man than Pete Aurbitter.

Dan reached out a big hand and caught Cluff by the collar, pulling him away from Aurbitter the way he'd pull a dog out of a fight. Cluff tried to lunge back at the Bell man but couldn't. Then he wheeled on York.

Dan glared at him and he saw in Cluff's eyes that he remembered what had happened the last time he tackled York.

'This is no place to fight,' York said sharply. 'Only a fool would jump a Bell man with Belling's whole crew here.'

Cluff nodded, the message getting through to him.

A Bell hand had appeared as if by magic and wrapped his arms around Aurbitter. 'Let's not spoil the fund-raiser,' he said to Aurbitter.

Aurbitter and Cluff exchanged a few choice insults while being held apart, but York had the feeling both were satisfied that the fight was over. Aurbitter was sure to lose and Cluff would be lucky to get out of the hotel alive if he beat Aurbitter.

The Bell man released his hold on Aurbitter. York thought Pete would back off but, instead, he caught Winnie by the arm and swept her out on the floor where a square was just forming. With a furious lunge, Cluff broke free from Dan and lumbered out on the floor in pursuit of Aurbitter and Winnie. Two Bell riders saw him coming and intercepted him just as he reached Aurbitter and the girl.

Even Cluff recognized the odds against him. While he blustered and roared his anger, Winnie slipped away and watched the proceedings like a spectator at a gladiator fight. York remembered how excited she had been when he had fought Cluff. With her, he decided again, it was a case of winner take all, including Winnie.

York wasn't close enough to hear what challenges Cluff might have thrown out, but the two Bell hands discouraged him from launching an attack right there. Aurbitter and the two Bell hands went toward the edge of the crowd, then to the back door.

York began moving around the edge of the crowd toward Aurbitter. With the tension growing the way it was, the quicker he got his information from the Bell hand, the better.

By the time Dan got to the spot where he'd seen the three Bell men, Aurbitter was gone. Dan did catch a glimpse of Cluff going out the back door. Maybe he'd go on home, York thought. It would clear the air here if he did.

Suddenly, the muffled roar of gun shots came from behind the hotel. It penetrated the noise on the dance floor. The music stopped as if the fiddlers had been shot. Being close to the rear door, York dashed out into the moonlit alley. A man was running around the corner of the hotel and York saw a gun still in his hand.

His eyes searched the ground for a victim of those shots. He saw him lying against a barrel that the hotel used for trash.

Men were pouring out of the hotel now. York was in the lead of the rush toward the man. A Bell hand raced past York, however, and turned the man over. York felt sick. The man was Pete Aurbitter.

'It was that Box F man,' the Bell man yelled. 'Let's get him.'

A stream of men ran around the corner of the hotel toward the front where the horses were hitched. York heard a running horse out front. Cluff had apparently grabbed a horse and escaped. He had driven a Box F buggy here and brought Carlita. The buggy would have been too slow for him now.

Most of the Bell hands got horses and went in pursuit, but the other people went back inside. Belling came in after turning the body over to the doctor. Belling and Gilda Wagasy got the dance going again. It was for a good cause. The enthusiasm, however, was gone.

It struck Dan that Aurbitter might have said something to his boss. At the first opportunity, York got next to Belling and introduced himself. When Belling recognized his name as the man who had shot Jeff Frake, he was all smiles.

'Did Aurbitter tell you anything about the buggy wreck up at the Trap?' York asked.

Belling shook his head. 'He didn't confide in me. I've wondered if he did see something since he was up there the day that the

138

wreck happened. But he didn't volunteer anything, and I don't pry into my men's business.'

'How long have you had a man guarding the Trap?'

'All summer on occasion,' Belling said. 'From now on, I'll probably have a man there all the time. Frake's going to try to break out of that valley and I sure don't aim to let him.'

'What have you got against him?'

'He's trying to horn in on my market here in Goldtown. He ain't going to do it. By spring, I'll have both of these valleys for myself.'

York turned to watch the dance. Aurbitter obviously had not confided in anyone so, with his death, Dan's chances of finding out exactly what had happened had disappeared.

He found Burr Belling almost as obnoxious as Sam Frake. The one difference was that Belling wasn't trying to kill him. But they were like two dogs in a fight over a bone. They would do whatever was necessary to get the bone, and they didn't care what happened to those around them during the fight.

With Aurbitter dead, Dan had no further interest in the dance. He slipped out of the hotel and went to his horse. On his ride home, he tried to sort out what he had learned. But uppermost in his mind was what he hadn't learned. He'd had an eye witness to the wreck at the Trap and the information had been whisked away from him. He was more convinced than ever that it had been murder.

In his own mind, Sam Frake was still the prime suspect, although Fred Cluff, Lennie Swift, and Omar Perkins could not be completely counted out.

Before going to bed in his new house in Nugget, Dan checked on the barn where he'd seen the extra horse. It was still there. That meant that Horace Trillingham's woman visitor was still here in Nugget. Tomorrow morning York would find out who she was if he had to do it at gunpoint.

That resolution dissolved in the first streaks of dawn. It had been late when York got back from Goldtown and he had dropped into a deep sleep.

When the first shot slammed into the side of the house, close to his bed, he felt as if he might not escape this assault.

CHAPTER ELEVEN

Rolling onto the floor, Dan reached up and pulled his revolver from under his pillow where he kept it at night. The cobwebs of sleep were being singed from his brain by two more shots that slammed into the house, one breaking a window.

Rolling to the window, he lifted his head just high enough to peek out. The dawn was staining the sky and casting weird shadows over the town. It really looked like a ghost town now. But those bullets were not being fired by ghosts.

It was still dark enough for Dan to see the flash as another shot was sent toward the house. York answered that shot, then ducked down and moved away from the window. As he expected, two shots slammed into the house just below that window.

Two shots meant that there were at least two men out there. He wouldn't be surprised if there were three. And all from the Box F.

Peeking out the window again, he saw a small man dodging from one building to another to get a different angle on York's house. The light was dim and tricky, but Dan fired quickly. The man yelped in alarm and dived behind a building. Another shot came from the first area where York had located the attackers. He got off a quick shot in that direction.

With both men seemingly pinned down behind two buildings on the creek side of the house, York moved over to another window to look for the third man.

Deciding there were only two, he went back to the other window and rapidly sent two shots into the areas where the two men were.

Reloading quickly, he moved to the door of the house and pulled it open slightly, glad that it didn't squeak. Moving silently to a corner of the house he waited, peering around at the spots where the two gunmen had been.

Suddenly, a big man burst out of his hiding place behind one building and sprinted for another house out of sight of the window in York's house. York fired quickly at him, sending him diving for the cover of an old wagon standing between the two houses. Wheeling, York was in time to see the little man moving out far enough to get a shot at him. Dan beat him to the shot and he dived back under cover.

The two men yelled at each other, but York couldn't make out what they were saying. Obviously, they hadn't expected York to attack them and they were not relishing the situation.

142

'Now!'

York heard that word and a second later understood what it meant. Two shots were directed at the corner of the house where he was standing. He ducked back as two more shots slammed into the same corner. A couple of seconds later, two more shots hit the house.

York waited, wondering if they would empty their guns before stopping. When there was a lull in the fusillade, he peered around the corner again. No shots greeted him. Then he saw two dim figures dodging away into the shadows along the creek. A moment later they appeared again on horseback, riding hard across the creek toward the open range and the Box F.

York sent one shot after them in disgust, knowing they were already out of range. That had to be Lennie Swift and Fred Cluff. He hadn't expected them this morning. He didn't think they would know which house he had moved to. Besides, Cluff had been in Goldtown last night. He would hardly be expected to be on a raid at this hour of the day.

'What's all the war about?' Vicarona yelled at York as he headed back into his house.

'A visit from the Box F,' York called.

It was time to get up, anyway, even if it had been a short night.

Fully dressed, Dan reloaded his gun and

headed out into the dawn light. Moving over to the barn where the extra horse had been last night, he was surprised to find the animal gone. He went directly to Horace Trillingham's mansion and knocked.

The Englishman opened the door and invited him into the front room. A quick glance around showed York that breakfast dishes were stacked on a big table. It seemed to him that the two had eaten here, but it was obvious Trillingham's visitor was gone.

'Those Box F gunnies have no respect for a man's sleep,' Trillingham complained.

'Your company gone?' York asked.

Trillingham nodded. 'Had to get an early start. Going back to Denver.'

York waited, but Trillingham said no more. From his experience with the Englishman the last few days, he knew he wasn't going to get any more information out of him. If he was going to find out anything, he'd have to catch the woman who had left here this morning. There was only one way she could go. And somehow Dan felt she was connected with his problems.

Leaving Trillingham, he hurried to the barn where he kept his horse. Saddling up, he headed for the narrow canyon between Nugget and Goldtown. He had no idea how much of a head start the woman had on him. It just didn't seem logical that a woman would start out alone before daylight, but she surely had left Nugget before Cluff and Swift hit York's house.

When he reached the top of the falls at the Trap, he still hadn't caught sight of any rider ahead. He realized he had little chance of catching up with the woman who had been at Trillingham's. If she was so determined that no one should see her, she might have started at midnight to be sure she got out of the canyon before she was spotted.

Riding slowly down the steep grade, Dan turned of at the bottom and went to the buggy wreck. Dismounting, he examined the splintered buggy again. He saw fairly fresh tracks around the buggy and stooped to examine them. He discovered then that they were his own. But somehow they gave him an idea. He knew he had to get out of Nugget or somebody from the Box F would find a way to kill him. Why not stay here below the Trap and see if he could coax the one who had caused the wreck to come here and give himself away?

It took him only a minute to devise a scheme that he hoped would bring the murderer to the falls. He'd spread the word in both Nugget and Goldtown that there was a message scratched on the floor of the buggy that might point to the person who had crowded the buggy off the road. When that reached the ears of the guilty party, surely he'd come to see for himself what it said. Dan would be here to greet him.

He found a rock and, in crude letters, scratched the words, 'I know you,' on one of the least splintered boards. He'd tell no one what the words were. Anyone who wanted to know would have to come and see for himself.

He'd get the word to Winnie Wagasy in Goldtown and have her spread it around. But the Box F was where he really wanted to plant the message, so he swung into the saddle and rode back to the ghost town.

Dan was met by both inhabitants of Nugget when he rode in. Horace Trillingham was as friendly as ever now that his lady visitor was gone.

'Where have you been?' Vicarona demanded.

'Down at the falls,' York said. 'Did you know that one of the two killed in that buggy wreck lived long enough to scratch some words on the floorboard?'

Both men were instantly excited.

'What did it say?' Vicarona asked.

'I'm not telling anybody that,' York said. 'I just want to spread the word, especially at the Box F, that there is a message scratched on the buggy floor. I'm hoping the killer will come to se what it is. If I tell anybody what it says, it might leak out and the murderer wouldn't have to come to find out.'

Vicarona frowned in irritation. 'All right,'

he snapped. 'Keep it to yourself!'

'We'll get word to the Box F,' Trillingham said. 'Might stir up a bee in that clover patch. That message sure makes it look like it was no accident.'

York nodded. 'I intend to see that nobody tampers with those words. They could bring the killer right to me.'

He went to his house, hoping Trillingham kept his word and told Carlita. Then about noon, he saw Carlita coming. Why depend on Trillingham when he could tell her himself? Dan met her at the ford.

'I see you're still here,' she said coolly.

'I won't be staying,' he said. 'They'll burn the town down if I do. I've been down to the buggy wreck. Found some words scratched on the floorboards of the buggy.'

She dismounted. 'Does that mean somebody actually caused that wreck?'

'Looks that way. Maybe you can tell Sam and see if he has any ideas about it.'

'I can try,' Carlita said. 'He has to be in the right mood or he won't listen to anything Mama or I say.'

York still felt the chill in her voice. It had been there ever since he had admitted that Winnie had been with him at the falls. Maybe Cluff had told Carlita some lies about him that she believed, too.

She walked toward Vicarona waiting at his house and Dan turned toward his horse.

After a quick trip to Goldtown to spread the word there, particularly in the saloon, he returned to the falls, surprising a guard that Belling had put there to prevent Frake from bringing his cattle through. But the guard didn't bother him. Dan resolved to stay awake and catch any visitor who came to the buggy during the night.

Sometime after midnight, weariness defeated his resolution, and he fell asleep.

Dan didn't wake up till the gray streaks of dawn were showing above the canyon rim. As soon as it was light, he went over to the buggy.

He was surprised to find new tracks there. They were flat-heeled shoe tracks, but that didn't rule out anyone who wanted to hide his identity. What amazed Dan most was the size of the tracks. One shoe was at least three sizes larger than the other.

Eating a quick breakfast, he saddled up and headed for Nugget. Neither Vicarona nor Trillingham could give him a clue to the identity of the man who had worn shoes of two different sizes to the wreck site. York was disgusted with himself. He had set the trap, then gone to sleep and failed to spring it.

'It almost has to be somebody from the Box F,' York said.

'I sure wouldn't say that within hearing range of anybody out there,' Vicarona said.

'I'm going to find out who it was,' York

said and swung back into the saddle.

Crossing the creek, he headed for the Box F, wondering what kind of a showdown he would precipitate if he showed up at the ranch. Before he had time to contemplate that, he spotted a rider leaving the ranch, heading directly for him. He reined up and waited. Frake would hardly come to him this way unless it was part of a trap. Within a minute, he recognized Carlita.

'I saw you coming,' Carlita said as she reined up. 'Mama thought it was Horace, but I knew it wasn't. Are you out of your mind?'

York explained about the odd shoe prints and asked if any of the men on the Box F ever wore shoes.

Carlita shook her head. 'They all wear boots. Can't work cattle very well in flat-heeled clod-hoppers.'

'Whoever it was, he was trying to hide his identity,' York said. 'But that proves the wreck was no accident. Your mother and my pa were murdered.'

Her face was solemn. 'It does look that way. I want to help you find out who did it.'

'Good. Everything points to Sam Frake. He didn't want your mother to come here.'

'I know. He hated her. Mama told me why, but that is hardly grounds for killing her.'

'Maybe he didn't want you to leave the valley.'

'He never cared that much about me,' Carlita said.

'Does Mrs Frake believe Sam is innocent?'

'Why don't you ask her? Mama takes a buggy ride in the afternoon every nice day, usually along the mountains to the creek above Nugget. You might catch her there. But watch for Pa.'

'Thank you, Carlita,' York said, thinking how beautiful she was and wondering if she could be changing her mind about him. The next instant he knew.

'I'm not worried about you,' she said, her black eyes snapping. 'But if Pa finds Mama with you, he'll beat her.'

She wheeled her horse and headed back toward the Box F while he turned up the gentle sloping valley to the spot where Nugget Creek ran out of a small lake at the foot of the mountains rimming the north side of the valley. The lake was a collection point for the melting snow water from the peaks, and Nugget Creek was the overflow.

Conifers surrounded the lake, with two patches of white-barked aspen up the slope from the lake. York could understand why Genevieve Frake came here often. This place was the picture of peace.

The sun was climbing high into the heavens when Dan arrived at the lake. He expected to have a long wait, so he was surprised when he saw the buggy coming shortly after noon.

This was the nicest part of the day. Late afternoon up this high would bring an uncomfortable chill.

York waited until the buggy reached the trees before he showed himself. Genevieve Frake was startled when she saw him, but that passed quickly as she pulled the team to a halt.

'Carlita said you were still around,' she said. 'I want to talk to you. What's your real interest in Carlita?'

York was taken aback by her direct question. He was prepared to ask questions, but she had turned the tables on him before he could say a word.

'To give her the inheritance that's coming to her,' he said. 'Also, I think my pa and your sister were murdered. I aim to find out who did it before I leave.'

There was no show of emotion in her face. 'Any clues yet?'

'Some. Everything points to Sam. Do you think he could have caused that wreck to keep your sister from getting here?'

'He has a terrible temper. It flares up, then fades. But he never forgives. He could have done it, I suppose, but I don't think he did.'

'Is he having bad trouble with Belling?'

Genevieve nodded. 'Plenty since Nugget died. Nugget was Sam's town. He sold his beef there. Drove the extras down to Goldtown and sometimes on out to markets on the plains. Sam sand Burr Belling threw their herds together to make that drive. Then when the mines played out, and the money panic hit us last year, Nugget dried up almost overnight. Burr saw his chance to steal our valley and our cattle, so he won't let Sam take any cattle past the falls. It's going to mean a war.'

She slapped the lines on her team and the buggy started moving away. 'If Renetta was murdered, I hope you find the killer,' she said. 'But don't come to the Box F looking for clues. You were there once and got away. You'd never make it a second time.'

CHAPTER TWELVE

Dan followed the creek down toward Nugget, taking his time, pondering his next move. There was even less doubt in his mind now that Sam Frake was the man responsible for the deaths of Tom and Renetta York. Genevieve Frake had admitted that Sam had hated his sister-in-law and that he never forgave.

York was sure that she would never admit publicly that she thought Sam was guilty, so he still had to find the proof that would convict Frake. Where could he find that, especially if he didn't go to the Box F to look?

Reaching town, he tied his horse in front of the house where he had been staying before he moved to the falls. He needed time to think and Nugget was as quiet a place for that as he could imagine.

He was mulling over his puzzle when he saw Carlita coming down from the Box F. She must be making her daily food delivery to the two residents of Nugget. He left the house and led his horse down to Vicarona's. Vicarona was outside watching the approaching rider.

'We go to Goldtown once every two weeks

for supplies,' Vicarona said, 'but we'd get mighty hungry for good grub if Carlita didn't bring us some almost every day.'

'What will you do this winter?' York asked.

'We'll store up enough to tide us over till spring,' Vicarona said. 'Ain't much we can do in winter except take care of our horses and eat and sleep.'

York thought that sounded like a pretty bleak existence. Then he turned his attention to Carlita, splashing across the creek now. She reined up in front of Vicarona's house and swung out of the saddle. Handing a sack to Vicarona, she turned to York.

'I didn't know you'd be here, so I didn't bring any extra.'

'I don't need it. I get to Goldtown almost every day.'

She left her horse standing and started walking toward the mansion. York fell in beside her. He sensed a thawing of the coolness that had surrounded her the last few days.

'Do you ever see anyone guarding the falls when you go to Goldtown?' she asked.

He nodded. 'There was a Bell man there yesterday, apparently expecting the Box F to try to get some cattle past the Trap.'

Carlita sighed. 'Pa was afraid of that. He's getting pretty worked up. Snow will be coming soon. Then he can't move his cattle. He's got fifty head of fat steers and heifers

154

he wants to sell.'

'What's he going to do about it?'

'I don't know. But I'm afraid somebody will die before it's over. Pa ain't going to sit there and do nothing.' She looked at Dan. 'He's also going crazy because you're still around.'

'I don't suppose he'll ever accept the fact that I shot his son in self-defense.'

'You know Pa better than that,' Carlita said. 'To Pa, there is no justification for anything that is done if it hurts him.'

'I thought he'd hunt me down like a bounty hunter,' Dan said.

'He will if he can't find any other way.' She kicked at a rock in the road. 'You cut him down pretty bad when you outdrew him that day you brought Jeff home. He hasn't got over that yet. He's sent Fred and Lennie after you several times, but they aren't that keen to face you, either. Just this morning, he upped his offer to five hundred dollars to the one who kills you. He doesn't care how they do it.'

'Did he give you the chance to get in on that reward?' Dan asked.

She turned to him, a startled look on her face. Only when his face broke into a grin did she see that he was joking.

'You know I wouldn't do anything like that,' she said.

'There's been a few times when I wasn't so

sure, especially after you made up your mind I was running around with Winnie Wagasy.'

Carlita's face flushed. 'I'm sorry about that. I asked Fred. He told me that Winnie admitted you hadn't asked her to come with you to the falls that day. In fact, she said you asked her not to come.'

'I didn't suppose Cluff would admit anything to my credit.'

She laughed. 'He didn't know he was doing you a favor.'

They were passing the empty church, which had two boarded-up windows. It stood about halfway between the house where Vicarona lived and the mansion where Trillingham stayed.

Dan stopped near one of the windows that wasn't boarded up. He didn't even glance inside at the empty room. His eyes were on Carlita. It was good to hear her laugh. It was a low-pitched silvery tone that sent a ripple down his spine.

He stared at Carlita as if he were seeing a new person. Merriment danced in her black eyes, teasing him. She had her sack for Trillingham in one hand and her hat in the other. Some black strands of hair had slipped free of the bun on top of her head and fallen down to frame her face with the soft olive skin and the vibrant red lips that suddenly tempted York like nothing else ever had.

Never one to thwart an impulse, he reached out and caught her in his arms. She gasped in surprise but didn't resist as he pulled her to him. The sack slipped from one hand and her hat dropped to the ground. Although Carlita was a fairly tall girl, York stood almost a foot taller, and he had to bend his head to reach her lips.

In the back of his mind, he knew he was entirely out of line, but he just had to kiss her. It wasn't in his nature to stop. It was as nice as he had expected, especially when her hands, hanging limply at her sides when he encircled her with his arms, hesitantly lifted to rest on his shoulders.

When he released her, she stepped back, her eyes twice as big as they had been. He waited for a violent reaction from her, but she simply stared at him.

'I'm not going to say I'm sorry,' Dan said finally. 'I wanted to do that.'

She still stared at him. 'Then you and Winnie really aren't...'

He shook his head. 'She says she likes big men. But I don't think I fit her description of big. What about you and Omar Perkins?'

Suddenly, he dreaded to hear the answer. It hadn't mattered so much a few minutes ago. Now it did.

'I haven't seen him since the fund-raiser,' she said softly.

'Should he have been back to see you

since then?'

She shook her head. 'Not really. I – well, I don't see him as often as I see you.'

'I'd like to keep it that way.'

She put a hand on his arm. 'But there's Pa. He's determined to see you dead. I never knew him to start something he didn't finish.'

'I understand he's also determined to see you marry Omar Perkins.'

'I guess he is.' Her black eyes snapped. 'But maybe I'll have something to say about that.'

Dan pulled her to him again and kissed her again. This time there was no hesitation on her part. Her arms came up around his neck and seemed reluctant to let go when he stepped back.

'We'd better get these things delivered to Trillingham,' he suggested. 'He's probably wondering why you don't come.'

She laughed, her black eyes sparkling. 'We won't tell him, that's sure.'

As they walked on to the mansion, another question came to York's mind. 'Does Sam know I'm here in Nugget?'

'No,' she said, shaking her head. 'He's been here two or three times lately and didn't find you. But he won't give up. He'll come again. You have to stay out of his sight.'

'I'm not much good at running,' York said. 'One of these days, he's going to find me.'

'I don't want that, Dan,' she said. 'If it's a fair fight, I know you can win. But I don't want you to be the one to kill him.'

He hadn't considered that. In fact, he had a lot of things to reconsider since Carlita had come to town today. A few minutes could certainly change a man's outlook on life.

After delivering the sack to Trillingham, they walked back together to her horse. 'When will you leave the Box F?' he asked.

'I don't know,' she said. 'I can't leave Mama.'

He could think of no argument for that. But he knew he still could not deliver Carlita's money to her until she was free of Sam Frake. He didn't want to deliver her inheritance to her and then walk away, either. Things were much more complicated now than they had ever been.

As Dan watched Carlita ride across the valley toward the Box F, Vicarona limped up to stand beside him.

'You'd better make yourself hard to find,' he said.

'If you're thinking about Frake, don't worry. I've been around here several days now and he hasn't found me yet.'

'He don't give up easy,' Vicarona said. 'I know him better than you do. He's been here twice in the last twenty-four hours looking for you.'

159

'Maybe he'll decide I've left the country.'

'He knows better than that. Unless Carlita gets those stars out of her eyes before she gets back to the Box F, he's going to know something is out of kilter right now.'

York was surprised that Vicarona had noticed anything different when Carlita came back to her horse. He was a closer observer than York had thought.

He heard a sound behind him and turned to see Trillingham approaching.

'A touch of chill in the air,' the Englishman said as he stopped beside Vicarona. 'Sam Frake will be pushing his beef out of the valley any day now.'

'Belling has a man watching below the Trap,' York said. 'It won't be easy to get past him. He can rush up to the Trap and spook the herd.'

'There'll be a war,' Trillingham predicted gloomily. 'You'd better be a long way from here before that breaks out if you want to stay alive.'

'A war between Belling and Frake won't involve me,' Dan said.

'You're hanging around the falls most of the time, ain't you?' Trillingham asked.

'I'll spend the nights down there.'

'You'd better get out of there. If a war breaks out, that's where it's going to be. Besides, Sam is going to look there for you. He hasn't found you here in town, so he'll start scouting around and he sure won't pass up the Trap area.'

'I'll think about that,' York said. 'I don't want a run-in with Frake unless I know for sure he's the one who crowded that buggy off the road.'

An hour before sundown, York headed toward the canyon again. He would follow Trillingham's suggestion and get away from the falls for the night, but it wasn't because of the Englishman's concern. He hadn't made any effort to avoid Frake before, but now he didn't want to face him unless it was unavoidable. Suddenly, the entire Frake family had taken on a new meaning for him.

Riding into the canyon, his mind was on Carlita. She wasn't a Frake, he told himself, but she had been raised a Frake. And they were the only family she knew. If he did run into Sam Frake and win the battle, he wasn't sure how Carlita would react. What she thought meant more to him than what he wanted to do.

Dan had followed impulses before that had gotten him into some tight spots – and out of some. But he had never had an impulse completely turn his life around like that impulse he'd had to kiss Carlita.

Reaching the bottom of the incline near the falls, he rode over to the wreck. The prints of the oddsized shoes were still clear in the dirt near the buggy, but there were no new footprints. He didn't expect any new ones now. Whoever the trap had attracted had outwitted York by wearing those mismatched shoes that no one would normally wear. They were meant to hide the identity of the wearer, probably someone who normally wore boots. Nobody else would come to look at the message on the buggy floor.

Reining down the creek, he found a spot in some trees close to the place where the canyon turned sharply to the left. This would make a good campground. As he dismounted, he looked over at the spot where he'd seen the Bell hand last evening. He saw nothing now, but he doubted Burr Belling had withdrawn his guard. Dan had no reason to fear Belling's hand, so he found a good place to spread his blankets, unsaddled his horse, then took out some food for supper. Belling's hand must be at a different spot tonight. Dan thought of building a fire but ruled it out. Frake might have a man watching this area, too. A fire would attract Sam Frake like a light attracted a moth.

As a precaution, Dan slept with his gun almost in his hand. Yet nothing disturbed his sleep until about morning. Then the reverberation of a shot bounced back and forth between the walls of the narrow canyon.

York sat up like a spring-wound toy, his hand gripping his gun. Dawn was just tinging the tops of the canyon walls, but it was still dark down here. Leaving his bedroom, he grabbed his saddle and slapped it on his horse.

As he headed toward the road, he saw a rider dashing up the steep slope leading to Nugget. York jumped to the conclusion that one of the Box F hands had sneaked down here and probably shot the Bell hand who was on guard somewhere in the area.

York thought of going after the rider but dropped the idea. It had to be one of Sam Frake's men. York reined down the road and went around the corner. As he turned more to the east, stronger light filtered into the canyon.

Seeing the camp – farther below the falls than before – where the Bell man apparently had spent the night, he reined that way. As he did, another rider burst out of the trees beyond the camp and galloped down the road toward Goldtown as if he expected to be shot from the saddle.

Dan wondered if Bell had two men down here.

He'd seen only one yesterday. Then he was at the camp and reined up. He found a man still in his blood-soaked blankets. He had evidently been shot in his sleep. He wasn't dead yet and York dismounted to see what he could do to help him.

The bullet had been fired from close range,

so there could be little doubt about its effect-iveness.

York found there was little he could do for the man, but he stayed and tried to relieve his pain.

He was still with the man when he died. Then, as York straightened up, he saw riders coming from the direction of Goldtown. Whoever had ridden out of here must have gotten to Burr Belling and his men. It didn't seem that Dan had been with the wounded man that long, but the sun was high now.

He had stayed too long; there could be no doubt about that. If Belling didn't know who had shot the man, he'd likely blame York, since he was here with him.

Running to his horse, Dan swung into the saddle, working his way to the bend in the canyon. Behind him, the riders pulled up at the camp. Two dismounted as York slipped around the bend.

Then Dan heard horses thundering along the road behind him. One of Belling's men must have seen him. Now they were coming after him, and there was no place to hide.

CHAPTER THIRTEEN

Kicking his horse into a gallop, York headed for the Trap. He thought of trying to get up to Nugget. Belling's men would hardly risk a war with Frake now by invading the upper valley. But he knew the riders would gain on him fast as his horse labored up the steep incline. They'd pick him off with rifles.

Before the Bell riders came around the bend in the canyon, he swung over close to the creek, using the trees there to try to hide his flight. Turning in the saddle, he caught glimpses of the riders coming around the bend. He counted four. Not the kind of odds he wanted to buck, especially since he had no fight to pick with these men. If that had been Frake's outfit, he might have stopped and made a stand.

As yet they hadn't seen him in the trees and he stopped his horse not far from the falls. Thinking of the space behind the falls, he decided on that as a hiding place.

He dismounted and, ducking low, ran toward the falls and dived in behind the water. Stopping, he peeked out. The men were still on the road. Even as he looked, one man went up the incline while the other three cut of toward the falls. Apparently, they had seen him go around the bend in the canyon and had reasoned that he couldn't have stayed on the road and gotten out of sight this quickly. One man was being sent up just to make sure. The other three were going to roust him out.

York retreated to the hole behind the falls. There he got a surprise. Running his hand into the opening, he discovered it was empty. Someone must have found the gold and taken it. He had no time to worry about it now. That hadn't been his gold, anyway.

Most of the rock near the falls was washed clean of dirt, but there was some mud in spots where only mist fell, and there York could see tracks that were not his own. Whoever had taken the gold had done it so recently that his tracks had not yet been wiped out by the mist.

From behind the falls he couldn't make out whether they were shoe prints or boot prints. He certainly couldn't venture out to see until Belling and his men moved on. The odds were they'd find him, anyway, York thought. He didn't want to fight with Burr Belling. There was nothing to be gained by it. Belling probably didn't realize that the man he'd chased in here was not a Box F man.

Belling and his men came close to the falls but didn't look behind them. Likely they didn't realize anyone could get behind the falling water. They rode by his horse in the trees, too, without seeing it.

When they got to the northeast as far from the falls as they could go without leaving the area, York decided his best chance was to make a run for it. Belling wouldn't give up without one more search. He'd find him or his horse the next time.

Trying to keep trees between himself and the men, Dan slipped out from behind the falls and darted over into the trees where his horse was still standing. Flipping the reins over the horse's neck, he swung into the saddle. Then he began moving quietly through the trees to the southeast.

But one of the men sighted him. With a yell he slapped his spurs into his horse's flanks and charged toward York. York was already nearer the open end of the enclosed area than the Bell men, so he reined his horse out of the trees where he had running room and leaned forward. The horse needed no urging. He stretched into his fastest run and dashed down the canyon.

One of the men behind York fired once at him. The distance was too far for accuracy and there were trees and bends in the canyon that kept York out of sight much of the time. His horse was a good one and, when he finally broke out of the canyon into the valley that surrounded Goldtown, he was well out of range of the men behind him.

York considered riding right on down the valley and out of the mountains. Once Dan was out of the valley, Belling would likely call off the chase.

Then Dan thought of Carlita and his mission here. He wasn't going to let Burr Belling run him out of the country even if he didn't want to fight him.

Swinging his horse in a gradual circle so that Belling wouldn't see what he had in mind and cut him off, Dan was soon heading toward Goldtown. If he could get there ahead of the others, maybe he could enlist Sheriff Heck Posey to calm Belling down and explain that York was not the one who had killed the Bell hand.

But before he reached town, he saw a rider burst out of the canyon to the northwest and race across the valley. That must be Belling's man who had ridden to the top of the falls. York's first thought was that he was going to be caught in a squeeze between this man and Belling's crew. But then he saw that the man was ignoring him and heading directly toward Belling.

When the man yanked his horse to a stop in front of Belling, the Bell owner brought his men to a stop. York twisted in the saddle to see what was going to happen next. Within thirty seconds, the messenger had spun his horse around and was leading the Bell crew toward the canyon. York was forgotten.

Dan reined up and let his horse blow while he watched the four men race into the mouth of the canyon and disappear. Belling had found something more important to do than chase York.

Gently Dan nudged his horse into a walk toward town while he tried to find a reason why Belling had suddenly changed his mind about running him down. He was still puzzling over it when he neared town.

Sheriff Heck Posey was at the edge of town. He apparently had been watching the chase. York noted that he hadn't taken a hand in it. He reined up in front of the lawman.

'Why didn't you come out and join the fun, Sheriff?' he asked.

'You were taking care of yourself. They tell me there's a dead man up in the canyon. I have to go see.' He squinted at York. 'They also tell me you killed him.'

'I didn't,' York said. 'But evidently somebody told Belling that I did.'

Posey nodded. 'Lennie Swift came charging into town about dawn this morning with a wild tale about you killing a Bell hand up in the canyon. He made sure Belling heard about it by sending the bartender out with the word. Al met Belling and his men riding this way and they tore off toward the canyon.

169

'Reckon I know what happened after that,' York said. 'Al wasn't with Belling, was he?'

Posey shook his head. 'He came back to town. Swift headed back up the canyon after Belling chased you out.'

York was piecing things together rapidly. Frake must have sent both his hired hands to get rid of Belling's guard near the Trap. Cluff must have shot the man, then charged back toward home while Swift waited to see if any other Bell man showed up. It had been Swift who had broken out of the trees and raced toward Goldtown. He had seen a chance to throw the blame on York and he made the most of it.

Suddenly, a new thought hit York. Frake must have sent his men to get rid of the Bell guard so he could run his cattle through the canyon pronto. With Belling and his men chasing York around this lower valley, the canyon would be unguarded. Swift might have thought of that, but he hadn't expected Belling to send one man up the canyon to make sure York hadn't escaped that way. If Frake was bringing his cattle down, this man would have seen them. That could explain why Belling had wheeled back toward the canyon when his man had met him out in the valley.

Quickly York explained to the sheriff how he had it mapped out. Posey listened intently, then nodded.

'I believe you. Frake has killed more than one Bell hand, I'm sure, including Kurt Doyle. He wouldn't bat an eye over killing another one to open up that canyon to his cattle.'

'There's going to be a war up there,' York said. 'You saw Belling take his men that way.'

'Sure did. I'd better get up there and stop it if I can. Will you come along?'

'Might as well,' York said. He wanted to find out for himself what was going on. He realized that Belling might still accuse him of killing his man, but not even Belling could deny the probability that one of Frake's men had done it.

The sheriff got his horse and they rode toward the canyon. York couldn't see any urgency in Posey. If he really wanted to stop the fighting, he'd get to the canyon with all possible speed. He rode more like he was heading for a Sunday picnic.

Before they had gone far into the canyon, they heard the shooting up ahead. As they neared the falls, Posey reined up.

'Ain't no way we're going to stop the fighting now,' he said. 'And there ain't no sense in us getting killed, too. Let's wait and see what happens.'

York shrugged. If the sheriff wasn't going to get involved, he certainly wasn't, either. He had no love for Sam Frake and his two hired hands, and Belling had done nothing to endear himself to Dan.

Five minutes after Dan and the sheriff halted, the shooting around the bend stopped. A few minutes later, three riders came around the bend and yanked their horses to a stop when they saw the sheriff and York. Belling suddenly pointed a finger at Dan.

'They say he killed Larson,' he shouted at the sheriff.

'You know better than that, Burr,' Posey said without raising his voice. 'One of Frake's men killed him so Frake could bring his cattle through here.'

Belling swore. 'I reckon so,' he then growled. 'Then they got me to chasing after him while they almost made it through.'

'What happened?' Posey asked.

'We stopped them,' Belling said with satisfaction. 'Frake had forty or fifty fat steers and heifers headed down here to take my market away from me at Goldtown.'

'Anybody killed?' the sheriff asked.

'Naw,' Belling snarled. 'I wish we'd killed them all. We killed some of their critters, though.'

'Didn't Frake's outfit fight back?'

'Sure they did, but they stayed back behind the herd. When Sam tried to push his critters down the road in spite of us being there, we picked off the leaders. That sure changed his mind.'

'Did he take them back?' the sheriff asked.

'That's where he was headed the last we saw. We should have gone after them and wiped them out. If he tries it again, we will.'

'Go easy on the threats, Burr,' Posey warned. 'I'll just ride on up and see how many cattle you killed.'

Belling's anger subsided. 'We didn't shoot all you'll find around there. A lot of the leaders panicked after we shot a few. Several fell over the edge of the Trap. Sam ain't got as many to worry about now as he had before.'

'I can't recall that you own this canyon any more than Sam Frake does,' Posey said.

Belling bristled. 'You figuring on stopping me from protecting my range? I made Sam Frake a good offer for his cattle, but he swore he'd own every head of my stock before spring. I don't know how he figures on doing that, but I ain't taking any chances.'

'You two can't go on fighting like a couple of range bulls forever,' Posey said.

'I'll tell you one thing,' Belling said. 'There ain't none of Sam Frake's cattle going to come down into this valley unless they're wearing my brand.'

Jerking his head at his men, Belling rode past Posey and York toward Goldtown.'

'Not much give to him, is there?' Dan said. 'None in Frake, either, I reckon.'

'One of them will be killed before this is settled,' Posey predicted. 'Not much I can

173

do. The law can't stop a crime, only deal with the criminal after it's done. Let's see what happened.'

They rode around the bend of the canyon toward the falls. There were nine dead cattle at the bottom of the ledge.

One Bell hand was still close to the canyon bend, making sure Frake didn't return with his herd.

'Frake won't get his cattle out,' Dan said. 'Vicarona said that he heard Frake is planning on Carlita marrying Omar Perkins, and then Frake will be in a position to gain control of Belling through the bank. What do you think of that?'

Posey rubbed his chin. 'Rather farfetched, I'd say, but I've heard talk like that. It could be possible. Burr Belling does owe the bank a lot of money.'

York looked at the dead cattle. They were all in a small area not far from the wrecked buggy but closer to the wall.

'What are you going to do about those cattle?' he asked the sheriff.

'They're Frake's cattle. He can do what he wants with them.'

The sheriff reined around and rode back down the canyon. York considered his next move. He had turned back when Belling was after him because of Carlita. She was still up at the ranch. Nothing had changed. He headed his horse up the steep road into the upper canyon.

He saw that things were in a turmoil as soon as he broke out of the canyon. Box F cattle were scattered over the valley. Normally Frake never let his cattle graze down there unattended.

Riding on to Nugget, he found that the turmoil had spread to the town. Vicarona and Trillingham met Dan near Vicarona's house.

'Somebody sure kicked over the beehive,' Trillingham said. 'Sam Frake came by here a while ago madder than a wet hen. He said we had to get out of the valley.'

'He acted like he thought we had something to do with Belling stopping him from taking his cattle down to Goldtown,' Vicarona added.

Dan York thought that Vicarona acted more upset than Trillingham did.

'What are you going to do?' Dan asked.

'Ain't decided yet,' Vicarona said. 'Nugget is home to me and Horace. We ain't done nothing to be kicked out for. Sam throws some big tantrums when he don't get his way. And he sure didn't get his way this morning.'

'Maybe he'll change his mind when he calms down,' Dan said.

'If he don't, we're going to have to move,' Vicarona said. 'We won't get to see Carlita anymore.'

That was it, Dan saw at once. The two old men lived for Carlita's visits. She treated them like family and they thought of her as a daughter. Both men were agitated, but Vicarona looked as if he were going to cry.

'Can't you convince Frake that you haven't sided against him?' York asked.

'Nobody convinces Sam of anything when he's worked up like he is now,' Vicarona said.

'Somebody's coming,' Trillingham said, shading his eyes as he looked toward the Box F. 'Maybe we won't even have time to gather up our things before we're booted out.'

York turned to look. Whoever it was, no time was being wasted.

'I'll have a look,' he said and swung back into the saddle.

As he rode away, he saw Vicarona scurrying into his house and Trillingham running toward his mansion. Gathering things to take with them, York guessed.

York trotted his horse across the ford, then nudged him into a lope toward the approaching horse. Within a minute, he decided it was Carlita. He didn't relax.

Something had to be seriously wrong for Carlita to be riding as hard as she was.

Reining up when he met her, he reached out to touch her arm. 'What's the matter?'

'Pa's crazy mad,' Carlita panted as if she had run all the way herself. 'He beat up Mama and threatened to beat me, too.'

CHAPTER FOURTEEN

'Is he insane enough to beat you?' Dan demanded.

'There isn't anything he won't do when he's as crazy as he is now,' Carlita said, her voice breaking into a sob.

'All because he didn't get his cattle through the Trap?'

'That meant everything to him,' Carlita said. 'Burr Belling beat him and he can't take losing.'

'What are you going to do now?' Dan asked.

'I'm going to get help for Mama.'

'I'll go get her out of there,' York said.

It was her turn to grab his arm. 'No!' she shouted. 'Pa will kill you before you get near the house.'

'If I draw him into a fight, Genevieve can get away while we're fighting.'

'No!' she screamed. 'He's got a big rifle he hunts deer with. He'd shoot you before you got close enough to see where he was. I won't let you go.'

His eyebrows shot up. He was a hundred pounds heavier and nearly a foot taller than she was, but he detected no doubt in her voice that she could stop him. He'd seldom been stopped by anyone when he'd made up his mind to do something, but he had the feeling he was going to be stopped this time.

'Some things have to be done,' Dan said gently.

'Not this. Pa has beaten Mama before. She'll survive. You won't if you go to the Box F. I won't let you go.'

'Just how are you going to stop me?'

She glared at him, black eyes flashing fire. 'I'm going to tell you something. If that doesn't stop you, then just go ahead. I don't care what happens to you.'

He simply stared at her, thinking he had never really seen this girl before. Her face was tense and she was breathing in short gasps. Either physically or emotionally, she was at the end of her rope.

'I love you, Dan York. If that doesn't mean anything to you, just go ahead and get yourself killed.'

He had known somehow that she was going to stop him. He hadn't guessed this would be the way. What she said drove everything else out of his mind.

'Well?' she said when he simply stared at her.

'I love you, too, Carlita,' he said, aggravated at himself because his husky voice revealed the kind of emotion he had never let anyone see before. 'I have loved you since the first time I saw you. I'm not about to do anything that will change your mind about me.'

He reined his horse around toward town. He saw Vicarona and Trillingham starting out of town on their animals. They must have been scrambling to get them saddled. Vicarona's saddle had a special socket instead of a stirrup on one side for his peg leg.

'What about Mama?' Carlita asked, her voice little more than a whisper. 'I still want to protect her.'

'If you won't let me go help her, I don't know what we can do.'

They met the two residents of Nugget on the town side of the ford. York put the question to them.

'I don't know how we can get Genevieve away from Sam,' Trillingham said. 'But we can sure do something to keep Sam from getting his hands on Carlita.'

'We'll hide her where he can't find her,' Vicarona said. 'Then we'll stand guard. If he comes close to finding her, we'll shoot him.'

'He'll kill you first,' Carlita said.

'Not both of us. We'll make sure we're on either side of him,' Vicarona said. 'He ain't dumb enough to start something with odds like that against him.'

'Soon as he gets over his mad spell, maybe he'll be all right again,' Trillingham added.

Carlita dismounted and Vicarona swung down, too. He patted her hand. 'Don't worry about your mama, Carlita,' he said softly. 'Sam has hammered her before and she always comes out all right. Sam always regrets it afterward.'

Trillingham dismounted and moved to the other side of her. 'When are you going to marry Perkins?'

'I'm not going to,' Carlita said sharply.

'Good for you,' Vicarona shouted. 'All he's got is money and that ain't enough for a girl like you.'

'I hear Sam is already pressuring Perkins to foreclose on Belling,' Trillingham said. 'I think he's using you, Carlita.'

'He won't anymore,' Carlita said.

She glanced at Dan and he could see that she wasn't ready to say anything to the men about the declaration she had just made to him. That was fine with him, but he felt a satisfied glow at the way she had told Trillingham that she wasn't going to marry Perkins.

'Somebody's coming from the Box F,' Vicarona said sharply, turning all attention to the west. 'Could be Sam.'

Trillingham stared at the rider for a minute. 'It's Cluff, I think.'

'It is Fred,' Carlita said. 'Pa probably sent

180

him after me.'

York decided that this would be the show-down between them. Since Cluff was alone, York almost welcomed the chance to cut down the odds against him. But Vicarona had different ideas.

'Let's hide Carlita,' he said quickly.

'No need,' Carlita said. 'He has probably already seen us. But he can't take me back if I don't want to go.'

York braced himself for whatever action Cluff started, but the Box F man splashed across the ford and rode directly to Carlita, ignoring everyone else. Leaping off his horse, he reached for Carlita's hand.

She pulled back.

'You pa says for you to come home right now,' Cluff snapped.

'I'm not going,' Carlita said. 'He's beaten Mama and he'll beat me if I go home.'

'That ain't the point,' Cluff said. 'He says you got to come home, so you're going to go.' He stepped forward to catch her hand again.

She leaped away from him. 'I said I'm not going!'

York stepped between Carlita and Cluff. 'Maybe you don't hear good,' he said in a steady voice.

Fred Cluff stared at York, as if seeing him for the first time. He crouched slightly, his hand moving back toward his gun. But there

181

it stopped. York could almost see things dropping in place in his mind. He had fought York with his fists down by the falls. He'd lost that one ignobly. He had seen York draw on Sam Frake and beat him so badly that Frake hadn't completed his draw. Cluff was no mental wizard, but he could see that he didn't hold any trump cards.

Slowly he straightened himself and glared at York. 'I didn't come here after you. I came after Carlita.'

'The only way you're going to get her is to walk over me,' York said. 'Make up your mind fast. I'm getting impatient.'

'I didn't come here to fight,' Cluff said lamely. 'But if I don't take Carlita back with me, Sam will skin me alive.'

'That's no hide off me. If Sam wanted her that bad, why didn't he come after her himself? He ought to know better than to send a boy to do a man's job.'

Dan watched Cluff closely. Those were fighting words, but Cluff apparently had already weighed his chances and made his decision. Holding the upper hand, York decided to take advantage of it.

'Which one of you on the Box F scared that team and caused the wreck at the Trap?' he demanded.

'I don't know what you're talking about,' Cluff said, backing off a step.

Dan advanced on the Box F man. 'You

know, all right. Who forced that team off the road and killed those two people?'

'I don't know nothing about that,' Cluff said, backing away again.

'Was it Sam Frake?'

Cluff shook his head. 'Nobody out there did it. It was an accident.'

It was Dan's turn to be shaken. Cluff was scared, but York could see nothing to indicate that he was lying. Even if he was telling the truth, however, it just meant that he didn't know that Sam Frake did it. Dan had thought Frake might order one of his men to do the dirty work. Maybe killing Renetta York was too important to Frake to trust the job to a hired hand. He certainly wouldn't tell anyone what he'd done.

Trillingham took Carlita's arm and guided her toward Vicarona's house. Vicarona followed them. Cluff started shuffling toward his horse, but York stopped him.

'You know that wasn't an accident, Cluff,' he said. 'If you can't tell a better lie than that, I'm going to think you did it.'

'I didn't!' Cluff said. 'I swear I didn't. It – it could have been Sam, I guess. Or Omar Perkins. Yes, Omar Perkins. He sure didn't want to see Carlita leave the country. He'd heard that this woman was going to take her to Denver.'

'Do you have any proof of that?'

'Ask him,' Cluff said eagerly. 'He had more

183

reason than anybody for trying to keep Carlita here.'

'He doesn't look like a man who could to that,' Dan said.

'He probably wouldn't dirty his hands with the job himself, but he had plenty of money to hire it done.'

The longer Cluff talked, the more certain he sounded. Dan wondered if Cluff was just trying to draw his attention away from Sam Frake or if he really knew something he had been keeping to himself.

'Where did you hear this?' Dan demanded.

'Down in the Lucky Strike in Goldtown,' Cluff said without hesitation. 'People get loose tongues in there.'

Cluff reached his horse and York let him go. Swinging into the saddle, Cluff reined his horse around and kicked him into a gallop. But he didn't head back toward the Box F as York expected. Instead of crossing the ford, he turned toward the canyon and Goldtown.

York watched him, wondering if he was so afraid of Sam Frake that he would not risk reporting back to him without Carlita. Or maybe he wanted to warn Omar Perkins that he had pointed a finger at him. Perkins and Cluff had appeared to be friends at the dance.

Cluff was definitely heading toward Goldtown, and Dan wanted to know why.

Turning to Vicarona's house, he poked his head in the door.

'Are you sure you can keep Sam Frake from finding Carlita?' he asked.

'You can bank on that,' Vicarona said. 'We know this town better than he does. We'll hide her where he can't find her.'

'Cluff headed for Goldtown,' York said. 'I want to find out why. I'll be back shortly.'

'Be careful,' Carlita warned.

He looked at her, seeing the concern in her eyes. 'Don't worry. I've got reasons to be careful now.'

He wondered if the two men would fully understand his reasons, but he really didn't care if they did. They'd find out before long, anyway.

York rode cautiously through the canyon. Cluff might lay an ambush for him. He had been humiliated. Killing York would be the only way he could redeem himself.

But there was no ambush.

In Goldtown Dan headed for the saloon.

'Did Fred Cluff come to town?' he asked, thinking belatedly that Cluff might have just kept riding to escape Frake's wrath.

Al said, 'He sure did. Came in here only a short while ago. Omar Perkins was here, too, and Cluff challenged him. Seems that Perkins has beat Cluff's time with Winnie Wagasy. Cluff said he was going to take Winnie and leave the hills. Omar said Cluff wouldn't as long as he was alive. Cluff would have gunned him down right there except he knew that the banker wasn't armed and I'd use my shotgun on him if he drew on an unarmed man in my place.'

'Did Perkins back down?' Dan asked.

'Not an inch,' Al said. 'He headed home for his gun. I don't like it. Perkins ain't my favourite person in town, but I like him better than Fred Cluff. And he ain't got a rabbit's chance in a coyote den against Cluff.'

'I was told maybe Perkins had a hand in that wreck up by the Trap. Do you think so?'

Al shook his head. 'Of course not.'

Suddenly, it hit York. Cluff was thinking faster back there in Nugget than York had given him credit for. He evidently knew that Perkins was courting Winnie and he jumped at the chance to point suspicion at Perkins, hoping York would come down and jump on the banker. That also got Cluff out of a tight spot right then.

'Where's Winnie now?' York asked.

'She left town on a high run,' Al said. 'She had some kind of bee in her bonnet. She seems to like have men fight over her, but this time she's scared. Must be she wants Perkins pretty bad and she knows he ain't got a chance against Cluff.'

This fight was none of York's business, but he did want to know for sure about Perkins's

186

innocence or guilt in the death of his father and stepmother. He left the saloon and headed down to the bank.

Omar Perkins was pacing the floor with a gun in his hand when York went in. There were lines of determination on his face. Dan knew he was going through with his battle with Fred Cluff.

'You're being foolish,' Dan said. 'Cluff's a gunfighter.'

'I know,' Perkins said. 'But I'll stand up for Winnie till I die.'

'What about Carlita? I thought you two were going to be married.'

'I like Carlita,' Perkins admitted. 'But marrying her was Sam Frake's idea.'

'Cluff says you had a hand in that wreck in the Trap. Anything to that?'

Perkins scowled. 'Of course not. Cluff's a liar!'

York couldn't doubt Perkins's denial. Besides, if he was more interested in Winnie than Carlita, he certainly wouldn't have killed Renetta York just to keep Carlita in the mountains.

'Just why are you switching from Carlita to Winnie now?' York asked.

'I've always liked Winnie, and when I got right down to thinking about it, Carlita would never do for a banker's wife.'

York's anger surged up. 'Why not?' he demanded.

187

'She's never been out of the valley. She'd embarrass me at a convention in Denver. Winnie won't. She's been around.'

York suppressed an impulse to smash the banker's face. Carlita had twice the class that Winnie had.

Spinning on his heel, he strode out of the bank and back to the Lucky Strike. Just as he got there, Cluff showed up on the porch of the hotel and yelled at Perkins. York turned to watch. Al came out to stand beside Dan.

Perkins came out of the bank as Cluff stepped into the street. Just then Winnie charged down the street on her horse. She had a Bell rider with her that York had seen at the dance. She yelled at Cluff. Already starting to reach for his gun, Cluff jerked his eyes that way. A Bell rider was a sworn enemy of a Box F man. Cluff realized his mistake instantly and wheeled back to Perkins. But that instant had given the banker time to draw his gun and aim. His aim was true. Cluff never got his gun completely out of the holster.

Winnie and the Bell hand reined up in front of the saloon.

Al nodded to them. 'Pretty good timing,' he said sarcastically.

'I intended it to be,' Winnie said.

'Thought you were Cluff's girl,' York put in.

'Why should I be his girl if I had a chance

188

to get Omar?' Winnie demanded. 'A banker is a lot better catch than a cowboy.'

York turned toward his horse, disgust surging up in him. Winnie Wagasy and Omar Perkins deserved each other.

Urgency drove Dan back up the canyon. He wanted to make sure that Carlita was safe. As soon as he was sure of that, he'd ride to the Box F and face Sam Frake. That would mean guns without words, he was sure. Even if he won, he'd likely never know for sure that Frake was the guilty party in his father's death, but he'd be sure enough that he could let the matter rest. If he survived, he'd take Carlita out of the mountains.

Before Dan reached Nugget, he knew something was wrong. Vicarona and Trillingham were down near the ford and they were jumping around like fleas on a hot skillet.

'Where's Carlita?' Dan demanded the minute he reached the ford.

'Genevieve came by in her buggy,' Vicarona said. 'She took Carlita. We didn't want her to go, but Carlita said she had to stay with her mother to be sure she was safe.'

'Where did they go?'

'They're circling the valley now, keeping out of sight in the trees,' Trillingham said. He seemed less agitated than Vicarona. 'Genevieve was badly beaten up and she said Sam was an absolute wild man.'

'When he comes here looking for them like he'll do,' Vicarona said, 'we're supposed to tell him they went to Goldtown. That should get him out of the valley. I've got work to do in my house.' He wheeled around and ran to his house as fast as his peg leg would allow.

'If they stay in the valley, Frake will find them when he comes back,' York said.

Trillingham nodded. 'We were hoping you'd do something about Frake before he got back here. Once he's out of the picture, Genevieve and Carlita can leave.'

'You think he'll come here looking for them?' Dan asked.

'Bound to,' Trillingham said.

'What will Frake do if he finds them?'

'Kill them both for running from him maybe,' Trillingham said. 'Genevieve says she never saw him so mad.'

'I'll find them first,' Dan said and turned his horse, splashing back across the ford.

He wondered if he should look for the buggy or Frake. Carlita would never be safe as long as Frake was alive. That seemed certain now.

Halfway across the valley, he saw a buggy coming toward him. It was not keeping in the trees as Vicarona had said Genevieve was doing. York headed for it on a gallop. Before he reached it, he saw Genevieve in the buggy, but she was alone.

190

'Where's Carlita?' he demanded, reining up.

'Lennie stole her,' Genevieve sobbed.

CHAPTER FIFTEEN

'Lennie Swift?' Dan shouted. 'How did he get Carlita?'

'Sam sent him out to search the valley while he went to town,' Genevieve said. 'Lennie found us. He has always been sweet on Carlita. She wouldn't have anything to do with him. Now he's got her. I think he's crazy. I don't know what he'll do.'

'Which way did they go?'

'Toward the canyon. Lennie said he was going to take her out of the mountains. He'd have taken the buggy, but he said his horse would carry double faster than the buggy team could go. You've got to do something, Mr York.'

'I'll catch up with them,' Dan promised. 'If I don't get killed, I'll bring Carlita back. But don't expect Swift.'

He kicked his horse into a lope toward the canyon mouth. His horse had already been run hard, so Dan held him to a steady lope. Since Lennie Swift's horse was carrying double, he should catch up with him before too long.

Swift would be expecting pursuit, so York had to watch for an ambush. The canyon was the only way out this valley and Swift had to get far away from Nugget if he intended to live. Even Sam Frake, who might kill Carlita if he caught her, would not tolerate Swift's kidnapping.

York began to worry when he had gone partly into the canyon and had not sighted Swift and Carlita. Had Swift stopped somewhere in the valley to hide?

Then from the top of the ledge at the Trap, Dan saw the two riders on the horse just turning around the bend in the canyon below the Trap. Dan was closing in, but he was still quite a distance behind.

It was slow going down the steep incline to the bottom of the falls. But then York pushed his horse into a lope again. He didn't dare wear his horse out, but he didn't intend to give Swift a chance to rest his double-burdened animal at all.

Turning the bend in the canyon, Dan searched for the riders, but they were not in sight. Around the next bend, he did see them maybe a quarter of a mile ahead.

Swift saw Dan and kicked his horse into a run. York urged his own weary horse a little more to keep up.

Three more bends in the canyon and York had cut the distance between him and Swift to a little more than sixty yards. As he came around the next bend, Carlita's scream sent him plunging off his horse.

He caught a glimpse of the two as he hit the ground. Swift was off his horse, holding Carlita in front of him, a gun in one hand. Dan had half expected something like this, but he hadn't decided how he would handle it. Moving up against the canyon wall behind a slight bulge in the rock, he gave Swift very little to shoot at.

York was stymied. He dare not shoot at Swift because of the risk of hitting Carlita. Swift probably couldn't hit him, either, but his horse was resting. If Swift could keep York pinned down for awhile, he'd have a rested horse for another attempt to escape.

York stretched his neck to look around the rock. That brought a shot from Swift, but it went wild. Carlita had jostled his arm as he tried to aim. It gave York an idea. He had every confidence in Carlita. Swift was not such a big man that he could hold Carlita quiet and still handle a gun accurately.

Moving out into the open, York began a zig-zag run toward Swift. The little man fired three times in rapid succession, but each shot was sent awry by the constant struggle and elbow-punching of Carlita.

York was counting Swift's shots. He had only two bullets left now.

He was within a few feet of Swift when the little gunman suddenly shoved Carlita aside so roughly that she sprawled on the rocks. Then Lennie brought his gun in line with

Dan at point-blank range.

York threw himself at Swift, his hand striking Swift's arm just as the gun roared. The bullet shattered a rock three feet to the left of York. York planted his feet and drove a fist against Swift's jaw with all the force he had.

Swift's head snapped back like a blade of grass before a whirlwind and crashed against the canyon wall. Slowly he slid to the ground. York watched just long enough to see that Swift was in no shape to continue the fight. Then he whirled to Carlita, who was already scrambling to her feet.

'Are you all right?'

She nodded. 'What about Lennie?'

York spun back to the little Box F man. He was still slumped against the wall. Stepping close, Dan reached down and plucked the gun from his fingers, then crouched to examine him. His neck was broken. Dan didn't know whether it was his blow that had done it or the smash into the canyon wall.

'He won't be causing anybody any more trouble,' York said, turning back to Carlita. He held out his arms and she came running into them.

'I'm so glad,' she said. 'I was afraid for you.'

'He wasn't about to hit me while you were elbowing him, ruining his aim.'

Suddenly, an explosion reverberated in the canyon. Startled, they both stared up in the direction from which the sound had come.

'Let's see what that was,' York said. 'You ride Swift's horse. He won't need it anymore.'

They mounted and rode up the canyon toward the falls. It was only a short distance, but it seemed to York that it took forever to get the weary horses around the bends in the canyon wall.

Everything at the falls looked peaceful enough except for the dust cloud drifting out of the Foolhardy Mine.

'Must have been in the mine,' Dan said. 'Look at the horses there. Recognize them?'

Carlita was already riding toward the two horses standing some distance from the mine, apparently having dragged their reins that far when the explosion rocked the area. York caught up with her.

'That brown one is Pa's,' Carlita said. 'The other horse belongs to Joe Vicarona.'

York verified that. The saddle had a socket instead of a stirrup on one side.

'What was Pa doing down here?' Carlita wondered.

York had no answer to that. He rode closer to the mine. The boards that had closed it to outsiders had been ripped away.

'That big an explosion had to have been set,' York said. 'It couldn't have just happened.'

'They're both dead,' Carlita said in a whisper. 'I just know it.'

York couldn't argue with that. If the two men had been inside the mine when that explosion occurred, he couldn't see how either of them could have survived.

'Here comes Horace,' Carlita said, nodding toward the steep road leading down from the top of the falls. 'He must know something about this or he wouldn't be here.'

York looked at Trillingham coming down the slope with more speed than wisdom. He surely had heard the explosion. As he hit the bottom of the incline, he turned his horse toward Dan and Carlita, riding hard. He jerked his horse to a stop then, staring at the mouth of the mine.

'I should have guessed what he was up to,' he said, his voice choking. Tears were running down his cheeks.

'What do you know about this?' York asked, helping Trillingham off his horse.

'I saw Joe making up a package of dynamite, tying the sticks into a bundle,' the Englishman said. 'He wouldn't tell me what he was going to do with it. He had it all planned. I can see it now.'

'Was Frake with him?' York asked.

Trillingham nodded. 'We figured Frake would come to Nugget looking for Carlita and Genevieve. He did. Joe told him he knew where they were hiding, so Sam demanded that Joe take him there. Joe got his horse. I

198

saw the bulge under his jacket, but I still didn't figure what he intended to do.'

'He intended to kill Frake?' Dan asked.

Trillingham nodded. 'It was the only way he could make sure Sam didn't hurt Carlita. We had decided we had to kill him, but only Joe figured out how to do it.'

'Did he plan to kill himself at the same time?'

'Probably, although he never said anything to me about it. There's something you ought to know. Joe was Carlita's father. That's why he was so set on protecting her. Joe and Carlita's mother were married for only a year and a half. There was a divorce. Renetta had to give her baby away because she couldn't keep her and work for a living. Joe never had any money to help out.'

York saw the shock on Carlita's face. She hadn't known Joe Vicarona was her father. Dan certainly hadn't guessed it, either. Yet he might have. She had the olive skin, flashing black eyes, and raven hair of her Mexican ancestry.

'Wasn't there some way Vicarona could have done away with Frake without killing himself?' York asked.

Trillingham rubbed a fist across his face to wipe away the tears. 'Maybe, but I reckon he wanted to make sure Frake was in the middle of that explosion. Anyway, he told me once he didn't want to live if Carlita ever found out what he'd done. You see, he was the one who scared that team and caused them to go over the road at the Trap.'

Carlita gasped. 'Why?'

'He knew your mother was coming to take you away to Denver,' Trillingham said. 'He didn't want to live if you weren't here. He hadn't figured on killing Tom York. He just hadn't thought that far ahead.'

Dan had had two bad shocks in the last minute. He was almost disappointed that it hadn't been Sam Frake who had caused that buggy wreck.

'Was it Joe who came down to look at the scratches on the buggy floor?' he asked suddenly, recalling the big shoe print.

Trillingham nodded. 'He had a big shoe that he put over his peg leg. He knew the hole that peg leg made would give him away.'

The pieces were fitting together quickly now for Dan. Vicarona had kept insisting that the wreck had been an accident. York could see why now. There was one piece of the puzzle that still didn't seem to fit anywhere.

'Who was the woman who was staying with you?' he asked, watching the Englishman closely.

Trillingham wiped his face again, but the tears had finally stopped. He stared at Dan, then at Carlita. 'You're not going to like it,' he said. 'You'd be better off just to forget it.'

York shook his head. 'I'm not that good at forgetting.'

'It was Elizabeth Norton, your sister.'

York stared at Trillingham in total disbelief. The Englishman shouldn't even know that he had a sister. If Elizabeth had been here, why had she hidden from him?

'She wouldn't have had any reason for being here,' he said flatly.

'This was her second trip,' Trillingham said. 'She came first about three months ago. She said her stepmother was coming up here to see her daughter. She offered Joe a thousand dollars to get rid of her.'

York was even more astounded. 'I don't believe it,' he said.

'I told you that you'd be better off not asking. Joe had already heard that Renetta was coming to take Carlita back to Denver. He was ready to do anything to keep her from going. So he agreed. Elizabeth paid him half the money then. She was to pay him the rest after he had done the job.'

'Why would she do that?' York demanded.

'You ought to know that your sister is a very greedy person. She said that Mr York really owned most of the property that she and your pa shared. If she was dead, then everything she had would go to your father. She figured on getting half of that sometime in the future. She didn't aim for her father to be killed. And she sure wasn't figuring on

201

their will giving a big chunk to Carlita.'

York was trying to absorb this shock and still think straight. 'Why was she here now?'

'She actually came to get her five hundred dollars back. She claimed Joe crossed her up when he killed her father, too. Joe said he'd tell you everything if she didn't give him the other five hundred. It was a stalemate for a while. But Joe won out.'

'Well, he won't get any good of that,' York said.

'He told me where he kept all his valuables,' Trillingham said. 'I was to give them to Carlita if anything happened to him.'

York stared at the mine, thinking of the two dead men inside. He had misjudged Jose Vicarona, never suspecting him of committing the crime he had come here to solve. As for Sam Frake, he had judged him right except for accusing him of the one crime he hadn't done.

'I see why Vicarona stayed in Nugget,' York said finally. 'But why did you stay? Carlita didn't mean that much to you.'

'I wouldn't say that,' Trillingham objected. 'But I stayed because of the gold from Ike Hamm's mine.'

York nodded. 'You found it and hid it under the falls?'

Trillingham shook his head. 'That's where Ike hid it. I found it some time ago. I got it out when I was sure you had found it, too.

You won't find it again.'

York shrugged. 'I'm not interested. I have a half interest in a small ranch out in the foothills.' He looked at Carlita. 'I've got a roll of money here for you, the inheritance from your mother. Everybody said I shouldn't give it to you till you were free of Sam. You are now. And the other half interest in that ranch is yours.'

Carlita seemed speechless after what she had been hearing. She stared at York and Trillingham.

'She's also got all that Joe had stored up,' the Englishman said. 'I'll get it for her before I leave.'

'You're leaving Nugget?' Carlita asked, finding her tongue at last.

'With Joe dead and you gone, there's nothing for me to stay for.'

'I'm still here,' she said.

'You won't be for long.' Trillingham nodded at York. 'He usually gets what he wants. And I'm guessing you're at the head of his list. I'm going back to Nugget and get Joe's valuables for you.' He turned toward his horse, then spoke to York. 'You'd better check in the mine as soon as the dust settles. See if there are any recognizable pieces left.'

York watched Trillingham mount and start back toward the road. Then he turned to Carlita. She was the only bright spot in this whole sordid affair. He knew it must be a terrible shock to her to find that Vicarona was not only her father but also the murderer of her mother. York found it hard to accept that Vicarona was guilty when he had considered him a friend. Even more shocking was the duplicity of his own sister. But he would be sure to keep her in line in the future.

'What are you going to do now, Carlita?' he asked softly.

'I don't know,' she said. 'Mama will probably sell out and go to Denver. She has a brother there. I – I'm all mixed up.'

York nodded. 'So am I. You're the only thing that I'm sure of.' He held out his arms and she came to him like a child seeking safety.

'But I'm – I'm part Mexican.' She pulled her head back to look up into his face.

'So what? Nothing wrong with that. I love you.'

She snuggled against his chest again.

'What are you going to do with your half of the ranch?' he asked after a minute.

'It seems like a shame to break it up.'

'It would be a crime,' he agreed. 'Shall we seal the bargain, my future Mrs York?'

She lifted her lips for the seal.

The publishers hope that this book has given you enjoyable reading. Large Print Books are especially designed to be as easy to see and hold as possible. If you wish a complete list of our books please ask at your local library or write directly to:

The Golden West Large Print Books
Magna House, Long Preston,
Skipton, North Yorkshire.
BD23 4ND

This Large Print Book, for people
who cannot read normal print,
is published under the auspices of

THE ULVERSCROFT FOUNDATION